Soundtrack

Soundtrack

A NOVEL

JASON REYNOLDS

CROWN
New York

Crown Books for Young Readers
An imprint of Random House Children's Books
A division of Penguin Random House LLC
1745 Broadway, New York, NY 10019
penguinrandomhouse.com
getunderlined.com

Originally published as an audio original edition by Penguin Random House Audio, a division of Penguin Random House LLC, New York, in 2025.

Library of Congress Cataloging-in-Publication Data is available upon request.
ISBN 979-8-217-23159-1 (hardcover)—ISBN 979-8-217-23160-7 (pbk.)
ISBN 979-8-217-23161-4 (lib. bdg.)—ISBN 979-8-217-23162-1 (ebook)

The text of this book is set in 10.75-point Warnock Pro.
Concrete wall texture by worac/stock.adobe.com
Spray paint art by by Valentain Jevee/stock.adobe.com
Music notes by Anastasiia Hevko/stock.adobe.com

Printed in the United States of America
1st Printing

The authorized representative in the EU for product safety and compliance is Penguin Random House Ireland, Morrison Chambers, 32 Nassau Street, Dublin D02 YH68, Ireland, https://eu-contact.penguin.ie.

FOR THE ARTISTS

CHARACTER LIST

Soundtrack is set in New York City, circa 2011.

Stuyvesant Grey (SG), aka Stuy:
18, narrator, drummer; lives on the Lower East Side; his mom still lives in Bed-Stuy

Uncle Lucky:
Stuy's uncle; Stuy is camping out with him

Alexis Brown:
18, bass guitarist; lives in the Albany Projects, Brooklyn

Dunks, aka Duncan Randall:
18, electric guitar; Uncle Lucky's landlord; lives on the Lower East Side

Keith Jr.:
horn player; lives in the Albany Projects, Brooklyn

Frankie, aka Famous Frankie:
13, band manager; lives in Bay Ridge, Brooklyn

Let the madness in the music get to you,
life ain't so bad at all . . .

—**MICHAEL JACKSON**

PROLOGUE

IF THERE WAS A MOVIE MADE ABOUT MY LIFE, IT WOULD start with me, Uncle Lucky, and his friend Spit in the kitchen of our apartment. I'd be six, and I'd have on my favorite red socks. The ones my big toes stuck out. Uncle Lucky would be explaining to me for the hundredth time:

```
                    UNCLE LUCKY
      Nephew, anything happens, you call 911.
```

Then he'd put one bullet in his pistol and spin the cylinder. Spit would take a long pull on a joint and let the stinky smoke float to the ceiling, while Uncle Lucky cocked the gun and lifted it to his head. Then, Uncle Lucky, with his finger on the trigger, would close his eyes and say:

```
                    UNCLE LUCKY
      Lucky, lucky, lucky.
```

And BAM! The title of the movie in big bold letters would pop up on the screen: THE STORY OF STUYVESANT GREY.

ALEXIS

Uhhh.

Alexis sorta groaned, looking around at Keith, Frankie, and Dunks.

ALEXIS

Dude. That's pretty intense, knowhatimsayin'?

Alexis stuffed his hand into the bag of chips we were sharing and pulled out a fistful. He passed the bag to Frankie.

KEITH

Right! I mean, damn, Stuy. You couldn't have just started your movie with you sitting at the buckets doing a count-off or something?

SG

I mean, that's how I would start my movie. *My* movie. What y'all would do is on y'all. But me, that's how my flick begins. What about you, Dunks? Alexis already said his would start with him stringing his bass and turning the amp all the way up. Keith told us how hers would basically be her in the bathroom mirror shaving her head.

KEITH

I said that would be part of it. Then after the hair was gone, I would pick up my horn. And then you'd get this dope shot of me—

ALEXIS

Yeah, yeah, we got it.

Keith screwed her face up and threw a fake punch.

ALEXIS

Dunks, what about you?

DUNKS

Aight, check it. It starts off in space—

FRANKIE

Come on, man.

ALEXIS

Dunks, dude, you're not an alien! Get over it. You're from the Lower East Side!

SG

Let it go, man. Just let it go.

DUNKS

I play like an alien, though. Right or wrong?

Nobody said nothing. We all just looked away like somebody invisible was calling out our names.

DUNKS

Haters!

He snatched the bag of chips from Frankie, who was just holding the bag but not eating any.

KEITH

Okay, okay, okay, what about you, Frankie? How would your movie start?

Frankie sat there for a second, looking around at all of us.

FRANKIE

Well, I guess it would start the day I met y'all. My crew. The band.

KEITH

You met me first, so technically the story starts with me. But I'll let it slide just so we don't make these fools jealous.

ALEXIS

Oh, please!

DUNKS

I used to give you money for pizza!

FRANKIE

I mean, what does it matter for anyway? We ain't making no movies. I mean, we make music. Matter fact, we make magic.

CHAPTER 1

OKAY, SO I ADMIT, THE WHOLE "UNCLE LUCKY PLAYING Russian roulette in front of me when I was six" thing was kind of intense. But it's true. And it's important because it was the moment that pretty much changed my life. So let me finish telling you what happened.

Spit took a long pull on a joint and let the stinky smoke float to the ceiling, while Uncle Lucky cocked the gun and lifted it to his head. Then, Uncle Lucky, with his finger on the trigger, closed his eyes and said:

UNCLE LUCKY

Lucky, lucky, lucky.

And then he pulled the trigger. But don't worry, no BAM! Just a click, and Uncle Lucky and Spit started howling like lonely dogs and laughing like psychos.

And then my mom came home. And then all hell broke loose.

Well, not really hell, because my mom just isn't the type of woman to come in the house and start knockin' heads, which Uncle Lucky should've been grateful for.

Because had it been anybody else, Lucky would've been turned inside out. But lucky for Lucky, he got all the rah-rah between him and my mother. My mom was the softy of the two, which is why Lucky, the crazy big brother, was living with us in the first place.

He was crazy, and not really the rent-paying kind, but was also like the protector of the house, so she let him crash. But when my mother saw Uncle Lucky, who by the way had been babysitting me since I was born (this wasn't the first time I saw them do this with the pistol), holding that gun, laughing his head off, and me staring at him, holding the cordless phone with my finger on the 9, she told him for once and for all he had to get the hell out.

And that sucked.

Why did that suck? you ask. It seems like Uncle Lucky was a bad influence, right? Well, yes, but he was my uncle. My mom's brother. He was nuts, but he was always there and he never disrespected my mom in any real way, because she was his baby sister. I know it sounds weird, but he looked out for us. And when he moved out, this guy Dom moved in.

But Dom didn't come right away, thank goodness. Mom and I had about ten years to ourselves, and that's when I learned to play the drums.

See, my mother, in all of her sweetness, was actually a mean drummer in a band when she was younger. Her and my dad, whose nickname was Bottom.

ANNOUNCER

`We are the Bud-Stuy Magic Dusters.`

A punk band. Mom said back then, punk bands were all about being tough, and since they were a black punk band, they had to be extra hard to be respected and not seen as black kids just trying to be white.

So they named the band after some old New York street gang, the Hudson Dusters, and threw Bed-Stuy at the end of it so white boys wouldn't try them, especially since my mother was such a chump. And a girl.

STUY'S MOM

And punk takes no pity on the pretty.

I always figured Magic Dusters had something to do with magic dust, though. Of course, my mother has denied this many, many times at this point, but I know she used to get high. Everybody did back then. And she played punk . . . come on! I'm young, but I ain't dumb.

By the time I was born, the band had already split, mainly because she got pregnant with me. Once she told everybody she was having Bottom's baby, things changed. Well, really just one thing—my father vanished. He didn't show up to any more practices. He wouldn't answer his phone. He was never home. Nothing. And instead of replacing him while my mom's belly was steady growing, they just decided to call the band quits. The Bed-Stuy Magic Dusters were a wrap, and so was my mother's music career.

Later, Mom heard that the boys in the band started another band, and all moved to California. She always believed the whole split was a way to out her and protect Bottom from his responsibilities as a father.

She said she always felt like the Dusters wasn't nothing but a boy's club with a girl drummer. I can believe that. I can also believe that Bottom might've been on the run from Uncle Lucky. Now, you would think that a woman who was a failed musician, and whose child's father was a deadbeat musician, wouldn't necessarily want music to play such a major part in her child's life. It's like people who work in politics, or people who are famous movie stars. They usually don't want their children to do that same thing only because they've seen all the ugly sides of the business.

The drugs, the wild parties, the lies, the scandal. All the stuff that blows lives.

But my mother took a different approach. She pretty much drowned me in music after Lucky left. I don't know if it was her way of trying to fix me after seeing my uncle put a revolver to his head a few times, or what. All I know is, once he was out, Mom started taping pictures of famous musicians and bands to the walls in my room, like Sly Stone, and Bad Brains, and Bob Marley. Always playing different kinds of music in the house, from jazz to blues to soul, and of course punk rock. And because it was just the two of us, there were a lot of dance parties and fake singing sessions where she'd be wailing into the hairbrush and I'd be doing (very embarrassing) steps behind her, singing backup.

She didn't really play much of the Dusters' stuff back then, though. Probably because it was too painful. But when I got old enough for her to teach me how to play the drums—around seven—then she started introducing me to their stuff, crappy cassette recordings of grimy live shows, mainly because she wanted me to hear what she used to sound like on the kit. Loud and fast.

Drumming started simple. We used the kitchen table as the snare drum, and our fingers as drumsticks. Once I learned how to keep rhythm, she started showing me other things, like how to use my hands and my feet at the same time. She would take pieces of tape and make X's on the kitchen floor. She would color one red and the other blue. Then she would sit in front of me with her hands out, like she was waiting for me to give her a double five. In her left hand she held a quarter, and in her right hand a penny. Then she would say:

STUY'S MOM

Red, red, red.

And I had to use my right foot to step on the red X three times. Then she'd say:

STUY'S MOM

`Blue, blue, blue.`

And I would step on the blue X with my left foot three times. Then it was:

STUY'S MOM

`Quarter, quarter, quarter, penny.`

And I would use my right hand to slap the hand holding the quarter, and my left to slap the hand holding the penny. We would practice over and over again, her switching up the patterns to make it harder.

It was like some weird, ghetto Dance Dance Revolution, except she wasn't teaching me how to dance. She was teaching me to use all my limbs at the same time. It wasn't until I was ten that I actually sat at a drum set. It was her old drums that our landlord let her keep stashed away in the basement of our building.

She put a red tape X on the hi-hat pedal, and a blue tape X on the bass drum. She put a photocopy of a penny on the cymbals, and one of a quarter on the snare drum. She had a box of sticks that she was saving for some reason, stuffed in one of her drawers. She gave me two and told me to get to it. It was the most natural thing I think I had ever done.

From there came playing in school. High school band isn't really the coolest club in the world. That's for sure. I mean, either you're the band geek, walking around with a huge black case carrying a trombone, an instrument that no one really knows or cares about in high school, unfortunately. Or a band dummy, also known as a percussionist, which is short for "I can't really play anything so they gave me the triangle and a shake-shake thing and call me a percussionist to make me feel more like a musician, when really I'm just a noisemaker." And if you're a drummer, like me, which is usually a cool instrument in bands, you were stuck playing marching rhythms and stupid "pat-pat-pats" on a snare, and that's it. Not exactly drumming.

Then there was the "in a band" guys, who usually walked around school with guitar cases, and since the high school band didn't have any guitars in it, that was a sign that people with guitar cases were actually in a band. A *real* band. Not some janky school band. School bands have recitals. Real bands have shows. But because my mother felt like it would be good for my drumming and would keep me off the streets, she made me join the school band.

But it wasn't pat-pat-pat for me all four years. My junior year, I ended up convincing the band director Mr. Rochester to let me bring my set in. It wasn't much. Just a bass, snare, hi-hat, and tom. It was all we could fit in our small two-bedroom apartment (the basement got too hot in the summer and too cold in the winter), and even that was still a bit much. Not to mention I couldn't really play loud at home, only because my mother didn't want our neighbors to complain to our landlord.

We couldn't afford to get kicked out. She had been kicked out of a few places when she was playing with the Dusters, but back then she said it was okay because it was all about the music, and you could always find a couch to crash on and a can of sardines to slurp down.

But with me, she said she just couldn't risk it. I loved the stories about her toughing it out, letting the music rule every decision, but I was glad I wasn't crammed up on no couch, and I was definitely not into sardines.

Mr. Rochester let me bring the set in and said I could leave it at the school for the year and practice there whenever I wanted, as loud as I wanted. The next full band practice, I sat behind the set and brought some life to whatever drab song we were working on. Mr. Rochester was so impressed that when our big recital came, I had all kinds of drum solos.

After that, high school changed for me. I was cool. I would walk around twirling my drumsticks, which of course, girls liked. I would make beats on the lockers, and my friends would freestyle, and before you knew it there would be a crowd of people, including teachers, who were supposed to be stopping the whole thing but couldn't because, well, what can I say? I'd be rocking!

Everything was sweet. Until February of my senior year, when my mother met Dom. Or as I call him, Dummy.

I didn't even know she was dating anybody until Valentine's Day rolled around. Every other Valentine's Day we had spent together, but this one was different. I came home with some sweetheart candy for her, but when I opened the door of our apartment, there were roses all over the place.

SG

```
What's with the roses?
```

I closed the door. She sat there on the couch with her face buried in them, sniffing like some kind of drug addict.

STUY'S MOM

```
They're from a man I work with at the
call center.
```

My mother traded in her drumsticks for a job at a 911 Emergency Call Center. She's the lady who answers the phone whenever you call with an emergency. I mean, it's not music, but she's got one of those soothing voices that works perfectly for a job like that. But I wasn't so sure about her dating a man with a voice like that. Seemed like a setup.

SG

```
Who?
```

I sounded more like a father than a son. I guess she could sense my concern. There had never been anyone else.

No one.

It was always her and I, and that's the way I liked it, and the way I always assumed she did. She never even mentioned other men. It was just us. Our house. Our drums. Our life. She leaned back on the couch and smiled at me.

STUY'S MOM

```
His name is Dom, and he's a nice guy.
```

SG

```
When you start seeing him?
```

At this point my mother started giggling. She stood up and walked over to me.

STUY'S MOM

```
Well, Dad, we've had drinks a few times
after work. That's all.
```

I felt relieved that it was only a few drinks.

STUY'S MOM

```
But tonight, he's taking me out to
dinner. Is that okay, Stuyvesant?
```

She only called me Stuyvesant when she was teasing. Any other time, it was Stuy. Or Big Head.

The truth is, this whole dating thing wasn't okay. Not at all.

But what could I say? No? To my mother? A woman who had sacrificed her entire life for me. The woman who had given me music. I couldn't say no.

She deserved a nice dinner, and I sure couldn't treat her to one, though I promised that one day I would buy her the most expensive dinner ever, once the music paid off. But that hadn't happened yet. I was only seventeen. And she was only thirty-five, which was old but not that old. Still young enough to have fun.

SG

Yeah, I guess. Do I get to meet him? I mean, I need to check this dude out if he's gonna be wining and dining my mother.

STUY'S MOM

Of course. He'll be here in a few hours.

She sat there for a second, gone, and then she started chuckling to herself.

SG

Why you laughing?

STUY'S MOM

Nothing. It's just that for the first time, I'm gonna have to ask you to zip me up, Stuy. Into a dress. It's been a long time since I've felt pretty, y'know?

She looked at her arms, covered in colorful tattoos done by some terrible artist, if not herself, back in her punk days.

STUY'S MOM

All these stupid tattoos.

She forced a smirk.

And that's when I knew she needed this date. I hadn't really thought about how she felt about herself, ever.

I mean, we always had so much fun together that it never really crossed my mind. But when she said it, it hit me—she needed a real Valentine's Day, not a pity night with her son talking about music and stuff. She needed romance, I guess, which grossed me out, but it was true. She hadn't dated nobody since my father. That was seventeen years of not having a reason to put on a fancy dress. One that would help her forget about back in the day, and the band, and Bottom, and all that. One that zipped in the back.

CHAPTER 2

MY MOTHER'S FIRST DATE WITH DOM, WHO BY THE WAY looked like one of those guys who counts the number of times he brushes his hair and doesn't feel comfortable stopping until he gets to a hundred, was good enough to turn into a second date. And then the second date turned into a third, fourth, and fifth date. The fifth date turned into weekend getaways, and those getaways eventually turned into Dom moving in with us, which pretty much turned into Dom thinking he could treat me however he wanted to. Like he was my daddy or something.

So we fought. Mostly because Dom was constantly on my back about going to college after I graduated high school, but I wasn't sure I wanted to go right away because I had always wanted to try to start a band, maybe record an album, do a tour. Do it the way my mother did. Whenever I explained this to Dom, he would say slick stuff like:

DOM

You're going to end up just like your father.

Which was really just his behind-the-back way of saying that I was going to end up just like my mother, which I guess to him wasn't good enough, even though he had no problem sleeping in her bed every night.

Of course, I never let him get away with any of those stupid comments. That good ol' Uncle Lucky would stir up in me and I would zap out, giving Dom the blues, shooting every cussword I knew at him. You ever yell at someone so hard that it feels like you're going to break your throat?

I know that seems like a dumb thing to say because you can't break your throat, but that's how it was. I would shout until I thought my throat was actually going to break.

The wild part was, my mother always took his side. Always. She would make me stop yelling and cussing, and even tried to convince me one night that maybe music wasn't the best idea. Maybe college was better, so I could get a good job. Or maybe I should try to do both.

STUY'S MOM

Dreams are dangerous, and bands can be trouble.

My mom, the one I grew up with? Nah. That wasn't her. I knew that couldn't be the way she really felt. She spent the last ten years telling me something completely different, about how music is everything. Strange couches and sardines.

I knew all this crap was coming from Dom, kissing on my mom one second, then putting all this pressure on her to make me do something she knew I wasn't sure I wanted. One time, I even heard them arguing. He was screaming at her and telling her she was nothing, and that he was just trying to save me from being nothing too. Bastard.

The last straw was one night. I had just graduated from high school, with a pretty high GPA, by the way. I got home, and Dom had taken apart my drum set, pushed it into a corner, and put a new television in its place.

First of all, I was upset that this dude even touched my drums. Second of all, I was upset that he had them all crowded up in the corner, broken down, like my instrument was trash waiting to be picked up. And third, I was pissed at the simple fact that, as far as I was concerned, this wasn't even his house! I wasn't his son! My mom wasn't his wife! So what the hell was going on? He had no right rearranging furniture and all that. But of course, my mother, all in love and sweet and whatnot, gave him the green light to do it all.

So it came down to a choice I gave her. Him or me. I know it sounds overdramatic, but I couldn't take this guy anymore. I just couldn't. So yeah, him or me. She hesitated, so I left.

Destination Uncle Lucky's. By this time he had a tiny apartment right across the Williamsburg Bridge, on Essex Street, and was working as an elementary school teacher. My mother used to always get on him and say:

STUY'S MOM

`You won't be lucky forever, Lucky. Gotta grow up at some point.`

And when his best friend Spit shot himself years back on an unlucky turn of Russian roulette, my uncle pretty much did just that. Grew up. All the way up.

The night was sticky and thick like most summer nights in New York are. Especially once you cross over into Manhattan, where the weather literally seems like it's tropical this time of year. Minus the awesome tropical stuff like trees and weird plants, of course. The kind of weather that makes you sweat that itchy sweat. Gross.

I got to Lucky's place around ten. All I had with me was some clothes in a backpack, a box of drumsticks, and a whole bunch of pissed off.

The lights bouncing off the pukey walls made me feel like I had on green-tinted shades.

I knocked on the door. The acoustics in apartment hallways are always crazy, and the knock sounded more like somebody let off a few rounds. No answer. I tried again, but this time I used drumsticks, and the door behind me opened. A tall, weird-looking light-skinned kid stuck his head out, music thumping from inside his place.

DUNKS

`You knock?`

SG

`Naw.`

DUNKS

`You looking for Lucky?`

SG

`Yeah.`

I was just a little bit freaked out. I mean, I was a Brooklyn kid. A brownstone baby. This wasn't my turf. All these people, and the yellow cabs, the old spots that sell Spanish rice, mixed in with the new bars filled with white boys in black jackets who look like they want to eat my face, and now this guy, a black kid who I could tell probably wore that same kind of black jacket, is just staring at me, and all I want is for my uncle to open his damn door. So I knocked again. This time, banged.

DUNKS

Chill, chill, man. Lucky said you were coming. He went to get some food, and he left me the key for you.

He opened the door to his apartment so he could grab the key, and I could see that he had a crazy setup in there—like all types of amps and cords and stuff. I could also see that he was a slob and he must not have had parents. But he didn't really seem old enough to live there by himself.

DUNKS

Sorry to be a creeper, man. I just had to make sure it was you. Stuy, right?

SG

Yeah.

DUNKS

Duncan.

He handed me the key and held his hand out for dap. Then awkwardly he corrected himself and said in what I could tell was his best cool voice:

DUNKS

Dunks.

SG

Word. What you listening to?

DUNKS

That's me.

He looked behind him like there was another him back there playing the guitar.

DUNKS

I call it Pluto Music.

SG

After the cartoon dog, or the planet?

DUNKS

Both.

His eyes went to my hands, the drumsticks.

DUNKS

What about you? You play?

SG

Yeah.

DUNKS

Gotta kit?

SG

Not with me.

Stupid. I obviously didn't have it with me. It's not like I could just toss a bass drum in my backpack. I thought about my drums—my babies—thrown all on top of each other and pushed in the corner of my mom's apartment. Just thinking about it put fire in my gut.

SG

Left it all in Brooklyn.

Before the conversation could continue, Uncle Lucky came galloping up the steps, swinging a plastic bag filled with those white carboard houses that Chinese food comes in. The ones with the wire handles.

UNCLE LUCKY

My bad, my bad.

He hugged me, out of breath.

UNCLE LUCKY

Had to run out and get us some grub, nephew. Figured you'd be hungry. Ain't want you to starve to death while you here and your mother blame me for it.

SG

She probably wouldn't even trip these days, unless Dummy says it's okay for her to worry about me.

Uncle Lucky bit down on the back of his jaw. I could see it knotting from the outside.

UNCLE LUCKY

I don't even wanna talk about him. You met my man Dunks?

Uncle Lucky gave Dunks a pound.

SG

Yeah.

DUNKS

We were just talking about music. He was telling me he plays set.

UNCLE LUCKY

Set? What set?

SG

Drums, Uncle Lucky.

UNCLE LUCKY

Oh. Plays? Yeah, the kid's got chops! Gets it from his mama. She damn near drove me crazy when we were kids. Banging on everything—the table, the sink, the floor, the cabinets, my head, everything.

He looked at me, and it hit him.

UNCLE LUCKY

I guess you 'bout to do the same damn thing, huh?

I didn't really know what to say, because as far as I was concerned, yeah, I mean—

DUNKS

Nope. He's not gonna do that in your crib, Lucky. You got summer tutoring with the kids in the morning.

UNCLE LUCKY

Since when you care about my work, Dunks?

And since when you tell my uncle what I'm not gonna do in his house? You don't even know me, I thought.

DUNKS

I'm just saying, man, when Stuy wants to play, he can just play over here.

SG

Oh. Okay. Better had.

CHAPTER 3

DUNCAN RANDALL—DUNKS—WAS THE SON OF THE LUCKIEST man in the world. His dad was some bigtime stiff, Wall Street dude who also had a thing for playing the lotto. But when he played, he never played sentimental numbers like his wife's and son's birthdays, or numbers that came to him in dreams, but instead he always played 2, 4, 6, 8, 10, and 12. Ten years ago, when Dunks was eight, those numbers hit, making his already well-off dad . . . weller-off? Well-offer? Whatever, richer. And also even more of an asshole.

Unbelievable.

According to Dunks, after Mr. Randall hit the numbers, he left his wife, but not before leaving her a fat check and buying half the buildings on the block, putting them all in Dunks's name. Then he pulled a Bottom and disappeared. I guess he thought he was doing Dunks a favor by leaving all that property to him. Like it would make it all okay. But what he was really doing was making it so that once his spoiled son turned eighteen, he would be stuck being the landlord of about fifty people, including my uncle. And now me.

When it came to school and stuff like that, well, Dunks didn't really do much of it. At least not in the regular way. I asked him when we first started hanging out:

SG

So you never sat in a classroom?

It came up because he asked me if I had been to prom. I told him all about my date, Monica Swan, and how fine she was. Dunks thought that was cool and told me he didn't go to high school at all.

DUNKS

Naw, man, school's for humans. Not for me.

I didn't even know what the hell that meant. And if Dunks had ever stepped foot in a high school, the one thing that would become clear real quick was that not everybody walking around those halls should be considered human.

SG

So how you learn everything?

DUNKS

My father saw to it that I got the info I needed—you know, stuff that would work for *my* brain.

Which to me just sounded like: My rich daddy got me a tutor so that I wouldn't have to go to school and be picked on like regular kids. So while normal teenage "humans" like me were bribing and cheating and sometimes studying our way through school, this dude was at home playing guitar.

Now, when I say playing guitar, I don't mean in the traditional sense. (I'm guessing you can tell already that nothing was traditional about this guy.) His guitar, an old Fender Stratocaster, soft pink with PLUTO written in block letters on it in red marker, only had five strings. On purpose.

I can't even begin to describe how he had it tuned. All I know is he said it was in tune with his inner alien, which meant absolutely nothing to me. But when he picked it up and plugged it in, he could do things on it I've only seen Hendrix do on old clips me and my mom used to watch on the internet. Dunks was wild, but he was out-of-this-world talented with his five-string, girly-ass ax. I mean, make-your-face-melt good. The first time I saw him play was the day after I moved into Uncle Lucky's.

DUNKS

We gotta get you a kit, man.

He was standing over his amp, his guitar slung over his shoulder. Dunks was tall and super skinny. Like, ribcage skinny. Sharp shoulders skinny. If you didn't know his real name was Duncan, you would definitely be confused about why folks called him Dunks, because even though he was tall, there was nothing about him that made you believe that this dude had ever even touched a basketball. He might not've ever even seen one!

DUNKS

I can just pick one up for you at the top of the month, whenever these fuckers pay me the rent . . . Not your uncle, though. He's not a fucker.

SG

It's all good, man. I'll work something out.

I sat on a green milk crate. I mean, Dunks was cool, but I didn't even know him yet and he was talking about buying me a whole drum set. Dude could've been a psycho. People who make those kinds of offers usually are.

DUNKS

```
You like it. I love it.
```

It seemed like a random statement to make.

DUNKS

```
Check it.
```

Dunks let the feedback moan from the amp, loud and piercing. It literally cut the air off in the room and made my head feel like it was going to explode. Then he hit the first string on the guitar and let it ring out. Then the second, and the third. It was all such a dramatic setup that I started to doubt he could really play at all. But then he went nuts on the neck of his guitar, his long skinny fingers flying over the strings, hammering them like he was trying to tap out some kind of secret code to the cosmos.

The whole apartment was filled with sound, and I swear I levitated off the crate.

I pulled my sticks out, and after a moment of trying to figure out what the hell Dunks was doing, I caught the beat and started banging on the floor and up against the crate. Bass and snare.

The jam session went on for what seemed like hours. I added a chair to my ensemble, and other little knickknacks to knock on that Dunks had lying around the room. I was sweating, working it out, and when I looked up at Dunks he was leaning back, his mouth hanging open, just seconds from a drool. His eyes were closed, his neck tight and veiny. He was gone, and so was I. And it was amazing.

And that was it. We were a band. It wasn't like anything we discussed. It was just one of those things that me, Dunks, and the music knew after that jam session. We were definitely a band. Okay, not a whole band, but the beginnings of a band. A damn good one too.

FOR THE NEXT FEW WEEKS, I was pretty much always at Dunks's place.

Whenever I wasn't at Dunks's, I was chilling out at Uncle Lucky's, usually on my way to sleep but never quite getting there because Uncle Lucky always made it a point to tell me as often as possible that my mother had called him and texted him and emailed him and whatever else to ask him how I was doing. She called me a few times too, but I always missed the calls because of Dunks's obsession with all-the-way-up loud. Not that I would've answered the phone to talk to her anyway. There was nothing to say.

SG

Was she calling to apologize and to tell me that she finally kicked Dummy out?

Uncle Lucky was sitting in a chair—which he made clear was "his chair"—grading papers, which seemed weird because it was summer, and watching MTV.

UNCLE LUCKY

Naw, she was just calling to check on you, kid. She's your mom.

SG

Yeah.

I tried to get comfortable on Uncle Lucky's concrete couch. I went from lying in an *r* to lying in a *z*, trying to find what was the most comfy. The *z* was the sweet spot.

SG

And what you say?

I tucked a pillow under my head.

UNCLE LUCKY

I told her you were cool, playing music with my nutso landlord.

Uncle Lucky didn't look up from the stack of papers he was holding, but he shrugged anyway.

SG

Well, next time you talk to her, tell her I started a band.

Uncle Lucky wrote a *B* on the top of the paper he was grading, then glanced up at me.

UNCLE LUCKY

You got it.

Me and Dunks played every day, just about all day. Most times when I walked across the hall to Dunks's apartment in the morning, he'd open the door wearing the same clothes from the day before, his pink guitar still strapped to him like he had never been to sleep.

His breath always smelled like coffee and tired, and he always looked stoned, even though he didn't smoke. Whenever we took a break from music, we'd walk down to the Spanish spot on the corner to get arroz con pollo and lime soda. This is also where we'd hold our meetings about the future of our awesome band.

DUNKS

Here's what I see.

Dunks was shoveling yellow rice into his mouth like a caveman.

DUNKS

I think we need crazy sounds man, like didgeridoos and kazoos and harps and stuff like that. Really take us out there, y'know?

SG

Dunks, where the hell are we gonna find a didgeridoo player? Better yet, where do all the harp players hang out? Ain't seen nobody dragging a harp around Rivington Street lately.

I pulled the chicken from the bone.

DUNKS

True.

Dunks sort of grunted with his mouth full. He took a sip of the lime soda.

DUNKS

You right about the didgeridoo, but

the harp—I could probably make one of those.

I shook my head. Truth is, I knew Dunks wasn't joking, and I also knew that he probably could've made a harp. It just wouldn't look or sound like one.

SG

Look, let's focus on the basics. We need a bass player.

Dunks closed his eyes like he was trying to imagine the two of us with a bass player. A trio. He nodded, I guess, liking what he was seeing in his own mind.

DUNKS

I like where you're going with this.

SG

But he's gotta be dope. I'm talking nasty on the bass. Know anybody?

Dunks looked down at his food.

DUNKS

Naw.

Then he picked up a chicken leg and started chomping the gristle off the knobby part.

DUNKS

Well, kinda.

SG

What you mean, kinda?

DUNKS

I mean, I don't know him personally. But there's this guy who plays in Union Square every Wednesday, Thursday, and Friday around one.

SG

So basically, you telling me you stalk this dude?

I wiped my mouth, rice bits stuck to the napkin.

DUNKS

No. I stalk his music.

SG

No. You stalk *him*.

DUNKS

No, it's just that I think he's an alien too.

I stared at Dunks with a blank face for a moment. I guess I was waiting for him to crack a smile to let me know he was joking. But nothing.

SG

It's official. You. Are. Nuts.

CHAPTER 4

ALEXIS BROWN WAS HIS NAME. THAT'S RIGHT, *HIS*. AND even though it would be easy to pick on him because of the whole Alexis thing, if you saw how big he was, you would quickly change your mind, and Alexis would suddenly seem like the toughest name you've ever heard in your life.

Dude was a giant. Maybe six-foot-five, well over 250 pounds. You could just look at him and tell he was born to be a football player, or a wrestler, or a bodyguard, but somewhere along the way somebody put a bass guitar in his hand. And me, Dunks, and everybody else standing in Union Square that Wednesday watching him play was thankful to whoever that person was.

Thunderfunk. That's the best way I can describe the sound. Alexis had his amp cranked, powered by some weird raggedy-ass hookup he had with a car battery and a whole bunch of duct tape. But whatever works.

He was slapping the bass hard, like he hated it. Like it had made fun of his name. There was nothing soft about this guy, and he didn't treat his instrument like it was sacred at all. He strummed and banged and hooked, two-finger walked and popped all over the place, making the most awkward faces. He went from constipated to having a stroke to drug addict to old lady shouting at church, all in about twenty seconds.

There was pain, there was pleasure, there was tight and loose and everything in between with this guy, and I think I speak for everyone who was standing there when I say it was one of the coolest things I had ever seen.

The crowd who watched him play was as big as the crowds are when tourists gather to watch the breakdancers, or the short dude who impersonates Michael Jackson. But for him, it wasn't just tourists. Everybody was watching. Even the skateboarders and BMX bike kids who practically live in Union Square were standing there checking him out.

When he was done, everybody rushed his guitar case to donate whatever loose change they could dig up, especially for such a dope performance. Dunks and I hung back, still in awe of him, watching as he nodded at everyone, thanking them for their nickels and dimes on the professional tip.

Once the crowd died down, we approached. Well, really, Dunks just ran up to him, pulled out like twenty bucks, and dropped it in his case.

ALEXIS

Yo, thanks, man, but who are you?

DUNKS

What you mean?

ALEXIS

I mean, I see you every time I'm out here, lurking around. And you always put more loot down than anybody else, knowhatimsayin'?

He twisted the tuning knobs on his guitar.

ALEXIS

```
So, who are you?
```

DUNKS

```
Who are you?
```

Over the three weeks that I had known Dunks, I watched him give homeless men five dollar bills, leave tips at the takeout (which is just ridiculous), and of course, there was that time when we first met when he offered to buy me an entire drum set. It was just the way he was. It wasn't because he was psycho or anything like that. The dude was just downright generous.

And most people I know just ain't used to that.

Dunks bounced his eyebrows, which made it even worse. The giant tightened his face and stopped twisting the tuner, and that's when I stepped in.

SG

```
Uh, he means, how long you been
playing?
```

I stood beside Dunks. Alexis's face relaxed. Thank God.

ALEXIS

```
Forever. Started in elementary school,
knowhatimsayin'?
```

SG

```
Word. You play with anybody else?
Like a band?
```

ALEXIS

Yeah.

He bent down, scooping up the change from the guitar case, and put it in a plastic bag. Then he put Dunks's twenty in his pocket.

ALEXIS

Me and my best friend.

SG

What's your best friend play?

ALEXIS

Horn.

He laid the bass in the long skinny case and snapped it shut. On top of the case was a bunch of graffiti tags, as well as a big sticker that read BASS IN YOUR SPACE. Dunks saw it and his eyes almost shot out of his face. I nudged him. He mouthed to me, *I told you*, and I nudged him again.

SG

When y'all play?

ALEXIS

We just be around, knowhatimsayin'? Here and there.

SG

Well, we wanna come check y'all.

Alexis stood up and held the bass case by the handle. He sized us up, me first, and Dunks second and longest.

ALEXIS

What y'all, like agents?

SG

Naw, we just fans.

I realized that the big guy was a little nervous and didn't really trust us. Especially since Dunks had been dropping twenties in his case three days a week for months. I would be a little freaked out by that as well. Hell, I'm a little freaked out by everything Dunks does, and I know him.

ALEXIS

Look, I gotta get back to work. But if y'all really wanna check us, we'll be back here tonight. Around nine.

SG

Cool.

As soon as he walked off, like a building with legs, Dunks said out of nowhere:

DUNKS

Told you he was like me!

It was like he had been holding his breath the whole time and finally exhaled.

SG

He's nothing like you. But he can play. And his partner plays horn. If the horn player is good, then we gotta try to get them both. And if we do . . .

DUNKS

Pluto Music, in full effect.

SG

Uh. Right.

WE CAME BACK TO Union Square a little after nine. Of course, Dunks had wanted to be back by eight-thirty "to get a good seat," but I knew better. I mean, how weird would it have been for us to be out there waiting for them to come and play? I'll tell you. Way weird. So weird, in fact, that we might've gotten some unwanted static from a guy three times our size. We had to play it cool, so we showed up a little late.

The crowd was already thick. And I could hear people calling out and clapping as the bass boomed, and the horn, like lightning striking sharp and fast, added the perfect complement.

We could see Alexis, obviously, as he towered over almost everyone, shaking and making ugly faces, looking like he was two plucks from shitting his pants. We couldn't see the horn player, but we could hear how good he was.

We slithered through the crowd to get to the front, bumping elbows and shoulders with date-nighters and lovebirds, and teenage outcasts with rings and studs in their faces, suits and skirts, and everything in between.

As we got closer, I could see flashes of a short bald-headed dude pacing back and forth, his cheeks puffed out, with a trumpet to his mouth. But once we got right up on him, I realized he . . . was a *her*.

DUNKS

What the . . . ?

Dunks reached over and grabbed my arm and squeezed as the bald-headed trumpet girl went off.

SG

I know!

My mouth was hanging wide open.

DUNKS

I think she might be an alien too.

SG

This time, you might be right.

After the show, and the follow-up jam of nickels, dimes, and quarters dropping into the guitar case again, we walked up and dropped our—well, really, Dunks's—offering into the case. Another twenty. I told Dunks right after they finished to let me do all the talking.

SG

Yo, y'all did your thing, man.

I reached for a five.

ALEXIS

Y'all really came back. That's wassup. I appreciate it, knowhatimsayin'?

He looked over at Dunks and nodded. Dunks nodded back, trying his best to play it cool. I could tell all the stars and asteroids and meteors inside him were dying to come bursting out of his mouth.

SG

Of course, of course.

My eyes darted over to the girl, who was blowing spit out of her horn. So hot. Her head was shaved down to a buzz, and she had freckles, which made her face the perfect chocolate chip cookie.

ALEXIS

Keith, I want you to meet these two guys. I don't know who they are, but they don't seem to be going away, so . . .

SG

I'm Stuyvesant.

I spoke up quick, holding my hand out to Cookie Face, whose name I didn't really catch, even though I know the big guy said it. I just didn't hear it. Too busy staring.

KEITH

After Bed-Stuy? Named after the hood? Nice.

SG

Yeah.

I pretended like I didn't hear the sarcasm in her voice.

SG

And this is Dunks.

I hitchhike-thumbed over to him. Dunks stood there scratching his elbow, silent. So awkward.

ALEXIS

I'm Alexis.

The giant man put one of his hands on his chest.

SG

Alexis. Got it.

I prayed that Dunks wouldn't laugh, because one snicker and we were dead, our faces turned to two more pieces of month-old gum on the steps of Union Square.

KEITH

And I'm Keith.

SG

Keith? Like—

KEITH

Like Keith, my father's name. I'm a junior. I know it's not as cool as being named after a neighborhood, but it's what I got.

She pulled the mouthpiece out of her trumpet, then turned to Dunks.

KEITH

Dunks, huh? You play ball?

Dunks didn't say anything. I elbowed him to snap him out of whatever trance he was in.

DUNKS

Ball?

I knew that fool had never touched a basketball. Or any ball.

SG

No, he plays music, the guitar. And I play drums.

ALEXIS

Oh yeah?

SG

Yeah. And we're starting a band.

DUNKS

We're already a band.

I zipped past that comment as quickly as possible.

SG

Right. But we need a bass player.

I looked at Alexis. Even though we were talking to him, he had squatted down and was going about his business scraping the change from the guitar case. Then I looked over at Keith.

SG

And I didn't know it until I heard you play, but we need a horn player too.

Keith scratched the back of her head, then rubbed her hand down her face, using her thumb to wipe the corners of her red mouth.

KEITH

Look, we ain't interested in joining nobody's band. We our own band too.

SG

Oh, so you don't need a drummer? Right. What band doesn't need a drummer?

I tried to sound convincing without coming across as a jerk. Alexis stood up and stepped forward. Real close to me.

ALEXIS

This band doesn't need a drummer.

It was already dark, but I swear when he got up on me he blocked the moon and it got even darker.

SG

Okay.

What else could I say? I took a step back and said it again, just in case the baby beast didn't hear me.

SG

Okay.

That was that.

* * *

ON THE WALK HOME Dunks gave me an earful, and there was nothing I could do but let him go for it.

DUNKS

"Just let me handle it, Dunks. Let me do all the talking, Dunks." What?

We walked down Third Avenue as Dunks waved his arms around all crazy, going on and on about how I botched the whole deal.

We needed those two—Keith and Alexis—to complete our band. I mean, sure, we could find another bass player and another horn player, but those two seemed to fit. It just made sense. It's what old people always say falling in love is like. You just know it when it happens. And me and Dunks knew it, but I did a terrible job at getting Alexis and Keith to see it.

DUNKS

Dude, you told the biggest man on earth, who also happens to be the baddest bass player I've ever seen in real life, and a girl trumpet player—I repeat, a girl trumpet player—that *they* need *us*! How could you possibly think that was a good idea, Stuy? I just don't get it. *We need them!* You seem like such a smart guy. I mean, you really seem to have it all together. But what you did back there . . . man.

Dunks stopped walking and stood in front of one of those food carts offering meat on sticks and a random assortment of Gatorade.

SG

I don't know what happened, man.

I decided to finally speak. We had been walking a while, and Dunks was really laying into me. People were looking at us the way people look at couples fighting in the street. So embarrassing. And I couldn't even be mad about it or try to defend myself. I blew it.

SG

I thought they'd be cooler.

I fanned away the burnt smoke from the street meat cart.

DUNKS

Chicken, please, hot dog bun, barbecue sauce and hot sauce. Want something?

Which let me know that he wasn't the kind of guy who got really mad about anything. I mean, he was disappointed, but he wasn't the kind of guy that could really ever be mean.

SG

Naw, I'm good.

I turned my nose up at the sight of raw meat cooking out in the open like that. I was always told to never trust that crap, but funny enough, the rich kid had no problem going for it.

Dunks took a bite and yanked and pulled at the tough meat. Red sauce—the combo of both hot and barbecue—oozed from the bun and gathered in the creases of his mouth.

DUNKS

Okay, so now we tried your way . . .

He stopped to try to lick the barbecue sauce away. He obviously wasn't the kind of guy who wiped his mouth. He continued:

DUNKS

```
Now we'll try it my way. I mean, you
were pretty much doomed from the get-go,
because you thought they were like you—
human.
```

He stuffed the last bit of the chicken-dog-kabob-thing in his mouth and mumbled something about how they were aliens like him.

DUNKS

```
So tomorrow, we do it my way.
```

Oh lord.

SG

```
And what's your way?
```

I tried not to sound worried, but I was. Big-time.

He licked all around his mouth like a child with one of those nasty mouth rashes. It was disgusting, and people walking toward us were clearly grossed out. Especially the ladies.

DUNKS

```
You'll see.
```

CHAPTER 5

***YOU'LL SEE*, HE SAID. *YOU'LL SEE.* I SHOULD'VE KNOWN** better.

The next day, Dunks came and knocked on Uncle Lucky's door at like nine in the morning.

DUNKS

```
Stuy? Stuy, it's me, Dunks.
```

I opened the door and didn't say a word. Zombies don't talk. And before ten o'clock, I'm definitely a zombie.

DUNKS

```
Okay, so today we work my plan.
```

He looked behind him into his apartment as if someone would want to run in that war zone to try to steal something.

DUNKS

```
And I know last night you told me you
had to chill during the day today
because Lucky said he needed you to
```

```
clean up the apartment. So just meet me
right here tonight at eight.
```

I just nodded. At least I think I nodded. I definitely moved my head.

DUNKS

```
And make sure you bring some sticks.
```

He put his two pointer fingers up to the side of his head like antennas. Weirdo.

So yeah, Uncle Lucky asked me to clean up the apartment. No big deal. He said I was grown, and though he loves me, if I'm not paying rent—which I wasn't—then I had to at least clean up. No problem, can't even be mad about that. The only thing is, it didn't seem like Uncle Lucky had ever cleaned the place up. Ever. But I had to do it.

Before I got started, I opened up Uncle Lucky's ancient laptop, which was the size of a suitcase. Okay, not a suitcase, but definitely the size of my mom's old VCR. All I was hoping as I pushed it open was to not see anything I didn't want to see. You know what I'm talking about. Luckily . . . none of that. I went to YouTube and looked up clips of some of my favorite tap dancers.

Yes, tap dancers. It's something my mother got me hooked on when I was younger. It wasn't about how dope they were as dancers, but what kinds of sounds and rhythms they could come up with. So I just listened to Sammy Davis Jr., Gregory Hines, the Slyde Brothers, and my all-time favorite, Savion Glover. Their feet were like drumsticks creating the most incredible beats, and I used it as inspiration to try different things when I was playing. Usually, drummers listen to drummers, but for me, this was better.

I turned the laptop up as loud as it would go, which wasn't very loud, and got to scrubbing. And boy, was I scrubbing. The tub . . . I can't even explain. Let's just say it would've been easier to just take a knife and scrape the gunk off like butter. That was the worst part.

That, and the fridge.

My uncle only ate takeout, so the entire refrigerator was crammed with Styrofoam containers. I mean, from top to bottom, neatly fit like Tetris cubes, was leftover junk. Some stuff old enough to turn green. Other containers had practically nothing in them. Maybe a spoonful of rice. A chicken leg. Chinese, Thai, soul, Indian. (You ever smelled old Indian food? Blech!)

After that, I straightened up the living room, then sat down on the couch to watch Sammy Davis do his thing. I closed my eyes and used my hands to pat my thighs, copying every beat Sammy was making. The stutter steps, the slides, hard and soft. Sammy was so jazzy. Gregory was more soulful to me. And Savion was straight hip-hop. Hard. Aggressive. Head-rocking. Savion was the man.

Uncle Lucky came home around four with, of course, takeout, and was so surprised by how clean the apartment was.

UNCLE LUCKY

`Damn, Stuy.`

He flipped through all his papers on the coffee table, each stack organized by date.

UNCLE LUCKY

`You really got busy.`

Uncle Lucky walked into the kitchen. I smiled, because I knew he'd be so excited to see the clean kitchen, especially the fridge.

I heard him yank the refrigerator door open, that weird sound of something being unstuck.

Then silence. I smiled, satisfied with my good work. Then:

UNCLE LUCKY

Stuy!

The door closed, and Uncle Lucky came stomping back into the living room, panic smeared across his face.

UNCLE LUCKY

Where is all my food, boy?!

SG

You have *got* to be kidding me.

At 8:01, I laced my sneakers and slipped three drumsticks in my back pocket. One extra, just in case. I had no idea what Dunks had planned, but if he told me to bring sticks, I could only imagine.

When I opened the door, Dunks was pretty much falling out of his apartment. He had his guitar slung over his back, and a pushcart with an amplifier, a car battery, some duct tape, a milk crate, a few buckets, and God knows what else in it.

SG

Dude.

DUNKS

Are you ready to do this?

Dunks wiped his forehead with the back of his hand.

SG

Yeah, as soon as you tell me what exactly we're doing.

DUNKS

Well, let's just say, it's an alien coup.

SG

A what?

Dunks put his hand on my shoulder like I was a little kid and he was my mentor.

DUNKS

A Plutonian takeover.

I know you're confused. I was too. So let me make it plain. What Dunks was saying—which I found out about twenty minutes later after several other weird metaphors—was that we were going to show up in Union Square and play our music in the same spot that Keith and Alexis—the beauty and the beast—were going to play at.

We got to Union Square around 8:20.

DUNKS

See, we'll start playing now, and when they show up to play at nine, they won't know what to do. They'll have to at least respect us!

SG

Or kill us.

Dunks lugged the pushcart up the steps of Union Square.

DUNKS

Won't happen.

What if nobody shows up? What if we can't draw a crowd?

DUNKS

Won't happen.

Dunks started unloading the cart, his loose tank top hanging from his body like a flag hangs from a pole on a windless day. He screwed and yanked and pushed and tightened until he finally rigged his amp the exact same way Alexis had his hooked up! I don't even know how he figured it out. He took the buckets out and tossed them toward me.

DUNKS

For you.

Then he gave me a few other random things that I wasn't sure what to do with. A plate. A plastic two-liter soda bottle.

DUNKS

And a cymbal.

He handed me a baking pan. Where the hell did he get a baking pan?

SG

Dude, I just don't think this is a good idea.

Dunks plugged in his guitar, turned the amp up, and let the feedback whine. He adjusted the guitar, hiking it up on his shoulder, curly brown hair sticking out from under his arm.

Dunks ignored me and just struck a chord. He let it hum, then looked at me like, you playin' or what?

Then he stepped forward and began with his usual out-of-this-world riff.

Damn.

His fingers moved over the fretboard, and he twisted and turned his body as if the music was bursting out of his skin instead of the speaker. I got myself situated behind him, while he played the riff over and over. One crate to sit on. Two buckets to play. The plate on top of the other. The two-liter wedged between them both. And the baking pan under my left foot.

People started looking up and coming toward us. I pulled the sticks from my back pocket and checked my cell phone. 8:34.

I took a deep breath. Here we go. And from the first hit on the bucket, the sound loud and clacky, me and Dunks fell right into a mean groove. I was trying something I had heard Savion do with his feet earlier that day. And it was like magic.

It was just like we had been jamming in Dunks's dirty apartment for weeks, but now it was different because we were in front of people, and Dunks knew how to perform. I mean, I don't think he knew he was performing, but his whole thing—his alien-ness—was something you kinda had to look at.

Before we knew it, people—a *lot* of people—were standing around us, most just confused at what they were seeing. In a good way. We didn't have a case open for change or nothing like that. Just doing our thing. And it was nasty.

I got lost in it all.

Totally forgot we were there to pull an "alien coup," until the crowd parted and Alexis came marching through. Keith was behind him, with another kid. Looked like he could've been her little brother. Alexis looked pissed, and even though I was shook, I kept playing, especially since Dunks showed no signs of letting up. It seemed like when they showed up, he really kicked it up a notch. His hand moved faster over the five strings, the sound both crispy and crunchy blasting through the amp, as he duckwalked back and forth.

The crowd oohed like he was juggling knives or spitting fire or something. Alexis turned and looked at the crowd, and what a crowd it was. Then he looked at Keith, who looked pissed but couldn't help but bob her head and squish her nose up like she was smelling something sour. And she was. That funk.

This one guy reached up and tapped Alexis on the shoulder and motioned for him to step to the side because he was blocking his view. Alexis and Keith and the kid with them moved to the side to watch.

It was time to do it. Really do it.

I did a drum roll—really a bucket roll, I guess—and on the one, Dunks tore into a solo.

To describe the solo would be like me trying to describe some kind of acid trip, and since I've never done acid, I can't really describe it. Just know that Dunks's hands were bleeding, and when I looked out in the crowd, everyone's mouths were wide open. It was like everyone was frozen in place, like Dunks had cast some kind of spell on everyone. Even Alexis and Keith, who stood to the side, zombies like the rest.

At the end of it, the crowd snapped out of the trance and erupted, clapping, yelling, bumping each other, making sure that they all had just witnessed the same thing.

Dunks looked over at Alexis and Keith and nodded. They nodded back. Then he turned around to me and nodded. I nodded back. Then we both looked back at Alexis and Keith and nodded together.

I know. A lot of nodding. But it was really a conversation. It was: I respect you. You respect me. We respect you both and would love it if you came and got in on this.

And believe it or not, they did. The next thing you know, Alexis was opening his case and pulling the bass out from it. Keith popped open the small black box holding her trumpet, the golden horn shining as she lifted the top.

The crowd started howling. I kept the drum rhythm rocking. Savion. Dunks muffled his guitar and strummed lightly, as Alexis and Keith stepped up. Alexis rigged his amp up to the same car battery and plugged in. Keith lifted the horn to her mouth and fiddled with the valves, stretching her fingers out and cracking her knuckles.

I couldn't believe this was really about to happen.

A Plutonian takeover.

Dunks, drenched in sweat, turned and looked at us all. He wiped his bloody hands on his pants, flashed a weird smile, and just like that . . . magic.

CHAPTER 6

SG

```
Yo, who is this little dude?
```

WE HAD PACKED UP ALL OF OUR STUFF, THE AMP AND THE buckets, the plate and baking pan. Alexis had put his bass back in the case, and Keith had blown what seemed like half a gallon of spit from her horn before putting it back in its black box. The young dude who came with her was counting and trying to situate a fistful of money that all the people watching us had given him to give to us. All dollars, no coins, which is partly the reason I was wondering who he was. I mean, the kid had our dough, and you never trust people you don't know with your money, no matter how young and innocent they look.

KEITH

```
That's Frankie. He my little man.
```

SG

```
Well, wassup, little man?
```

Frankie, dressed in black skinny jeans, a black tee, and an Orioles fitted cap on his head, looked up at me.

FRANKIE

Wassup.

SG

He like your little brother or something?

KEITH

Something like that.

She squatted to tie her shoe. She yanked the laces tight, then pulled all the ones at the top of the shoe loose, which I thought was weird. Then she tied a tiny bow. No bunny-bunny ears flopping. Just a small knot you could barely see.

DUNKS

Do he play an instrument?

Dunks came out of nowhere, like he had just returned to earth.

ALEXIS

Don't matter if he play an instrument.

Alexis and Keith traded positions. She stood back up, finished with her sneakers, as he knelt and put a cuff in his pants. Crazy a guy his size could find pants that were still too long.

ALEXIS

The band is closed. No more spots, knowhatimsayin'?

I looked at Dunks, who looked at me with the biggest cheese on his face.

DUNKS

I told you!

He hooted, purposely bumping into me.

DUNKS

I told you!

SG

Okay, okay.

I tried to downplay it a little. I mean, they were still with us. Standing right in front of us. He couldn't have just waited until later to brag?

KEITH

Told you what?

SG

Nothing.

DUNKS

I told you, Stuy!

This time Dunks put his fingers up to his head, doing the whole "alien antenna" thing again.

Killing me.

SG

Okay, Dunks basically knew that once y'all heard us play, y'all would be down.

Alexis sorta jerked his head back like those old people who say things like, "The nerve . . ." But he didn't do that. That would've been . . . uh . . . different.

ALEXIS

Well, at first, I was gonna come up here and kick over the amp. Totally bash your whole setup.

The nerve . . .

SG

Yeah, that's kinda what I figured would happen.

ALEXIS

I mean, the whole thing was mad disrespectful, knowhatimsayin'?

SG

I agree.

I still didn't want to ruffle any feathers.

ALEXIS

I was like, "These cats are clearly crazy."

He picked up his bass. Frankie walked around and gave each of us our cut of the money. It came to eighteen dollars a piece. When he got to Dunks, Dunks folded the money into a hustler knot and gave it back to Frankie. Frankie was confused but smart enough to know not to give it back.

ALEXIS

But then when I started to really listen, I was like, "Oh . . . okay."

Alexis stuffed his money in his pocket.

KEITH

Yeah, I can't front. Y'all got chops.

Keith rolled her money into what looked like a cash cigarette and tucked it into her bra. She was so boyish, but so hot at the same time.

KEITH

Real recognize real.

ALEXIS

Right.

DUNKS

Told you.

SG

I know, man, dang. You told me. You told me.

We walked down Fourteenth for pizza, talking about what had happened and just trying to get to know each other a little better. More you know about a person, the better you play with them. I don't know if that's really true, but it sounds good, so I choose to believe it.

So we all started asking each other questions. Alexis's and

Keith's biggest question—what they really wanted to wrap their heads around—was why Dunks's guitar only had five strings.

DUNKS

'Cause I only got five fingers.

FRANKIE

You got ten fingers.

DUNKS

I know. But I mean . . . right . . . but . . . only five that work the neck and five that work the body. It's hard to explain. It's all based around this music I'm creating. Pluto Music.

KEITH

After the planet or the cartoon?

SG

Both.

I made the crazy sign with my finger up my head.

DUNKS

Whatever, Stuy.

Dunks pulled the door of the pizza shop open.

ALEXIS

Look, I don't care if your guitar has no strings! You could have shoelaces hooked up to that thing, as long as you can do what you did tonight, knowhatimsayin'?

Alexis set his bass case down on the seat at the booth in the corner. We ordered and used the money we had just made to pay for it all, which was nice. I got two regulars, Alexis got three regulars, Keith got two regulars, Frankie got a pepperoni.

DUNKS

Boss, I need an anchovy. Well done.

SG

No one ever orders anchovy. Nobody.

Then we all squeezed in the corner booth, folded our slices in half, and held them up above our heads so the grease and cheese could drip right into our mouths. Nothing like pizza after playing. Hell, nothing like pizza, period.

KEITH

What about you, Stuy?

Keith had a thin string of cheese dangling from her bottom lip.

SG

What about me?

I gasped and fanned air into my open mouth, hoping the burning cheese would cool down before it left that scratchy feeling on the roof of it.

KEITH

Never heard that beat you played before.

Keith, watching me struggle to swallow, blew on her slice before taking another bite.

KEITH

Just made it up?

Seeing that cheese on her mouth made me self-conscious about my own, so I reached for a napkin. The napkins in pizza shops are always the same as the paper towels in public bathrooms. Those brown stiff ones that feel like sandpaper, like you're gonna wipe the skin off your mouth right along with the marinara sauce.

SG

Naw. I got it from Savion Glover.

FRANKIE

Savion Glover?

Frankie pulled the cheese off his slice with his hand.

FRANKIE

He's a dancer, not a drummer.

ALEXIS

And you're Albert Einstein.

FRANKIE

Shut up.

Keith popped Alexis on the arm, but there's no way he felt it.

SG

But see, he was a drummer first.

Most people didn't know that about Savion. So I always got a kick out of saying it.

SG

```
So what I do is pull up old clips and
listen to his feet, to the rhythm, and
try to copy it. What you heard tonight
was the first ten seconds of when he
performed at the White House a long
time ago.
```

I looked around the table. I couldn't tell if they were all in shock at how awesome that was, or just totally confused. I shrugged.

SG

```
Just YouTube it.
```

Then I fired back, since we seemed to be interviewing each other:

SG

```
Why'd you pick up the horn, Keith? Not to
be like that or nothing, but I've never
seen a girl play the horn. And real
talk, I've never seen many dudes play it
as good as you.
```

Keith put her crust on Alexis's plate and took a sip of her soda.

KEITH

```
It was the last instrument left.
```

SG

```
What you mean?
```

KEITH

```
I mean, I didn't have a choice. When I
was a kid, I went to this music school
in my neighborhood. My parents were all
about making sure that I had something
creative to do because we lived in
the Albany projects. Maybe my mother
should've named me Albany. That works,
right, Stuy?
```

SG

```
You got jokes. Whatever. Just finish the
story.
```

It seemed like we already knew each other. All of us. Like this was the hundredth time meeting in this pizza shop, sitting at the big booth in the corner.

KEITH

```
Alright, alright. Anyway, they just
felt like the music would keep me
focused and—
```

SG

```
And out of trouble.
```

I finished the sentence for her. All moms kicked that whole "music will keep you out of trouble." Yet so many great musicians grow up, get famous, and get in so much trouble. Stupid.

KEITH

Exactly. So, instead of coming home after class, I had to go to Ms. Colick's Music School, which was pretty much a musical prison for kids.

ALEXIS

It was like slavery.

Alexis crunched on Keith's crust.

KEITH

I met this big fool there.

She laid her head on his huge shoulder.

KEITH

Thank God for that. Without him, who knows what would've happened.

Dunks had slurped to the bottom of his soda, and after realizing there was no more left, popped the top off and started shaking the ice into his mouth. Frankie just stared at him like he was crazy.

KEITH

So the way Ms. Colick had it set up is your parents didn't have to buy instruments, which was a good thing because if that was the case, I was going to be a tambourine player.

ALEXIS

Or a hand clapper. "Keith Ross Jr., on hands!"

KEITH

Hell yeah. Luckily, Ms. Colick had enough instruments to rent. But the issue was if you came later in the school year, a lot of the cool instruments were already chosen. Like the drums or the piano or the guitar.

ALEXIS

Or the bass.

Alexis slapped his hand against his chest.

KEITH

Wasn't nobody trying to play the bass but your big ass. We were kids. You were the only person who could even lift that thing.

We all laughed.

KEITH

Anyway, I came later in the year, and all that was left was the xylophone and the horn. And clearly, there's no such thing as rocking the xylophone.

DUNKS

I don't know about that.

Dunks's top lip was wet from tipping his cup up.

KEITH

When you're seven, no way. So I picked up the horn. Old Colick was crazy, but I'm thankful for it now.

ALEXIS

Colick was definitely crazy.

Alexis put his hand over his mouth to protect us all from a monstrous belch. He blew it out and fanned his mouth gas away from us. Thank God.

ALEXIS

She used to have us in there practicing like we didn't just come from school. I mean, it was nuts. We got there, got our homework done, and then practiced until we just couldn't anymore. No playing around. She was like the Joe Jackson of the neighborhood, knowhatimsayin'?

KEITH

She really was.

Keith picked at her second slice.

KEITH

Besides Terrence Cunningham, who chose the guitar because his daddy and his grandma played, you were the only other kid there who had some kind of real reason for choosing your instrument.

DUNKS

And what was that?

Frankie gathered the grease-stained white paper plates and stacked them up, Keith's on top with her leftover slice. He then took one of those hard napkins and wiped the crumbs off the table. Keith's "little dude" had good home training.

ALEXIS

Because my parents are deaf.

I looked at Dunks. He looked at me.

ALEXIS

So I chose the bass because Ms. Colick said it was the only instrument that they could feel—like *feel* feel. If I turned the amp up, it would, like, rumble through the apartment, and they could feel it in the way we can hear it, knowhatimsayin'?

I definitely knew what he was saying. I also now understood why he asked that so much.

SG

Wow. It's like another form of sign language.

DUNKS

But it uses vibrations. Spooky.

This time he was actually spot-on.

ALEXIS

Exactly. So that's what I chose.

KEITH

But the fool can't speak a lick of sign language. Thank goodness his folks can read lips!

ALEXIS

I can too speak sign language. See?

He put his middle finger up.

AFTER PIZZA, ME, DUNKS, and Alexis decided to walk back to Union Square. Keith had to jet and take Frankie back home.

KEITH

He's gotta be in before midnight, and he lives out in Bay Ridge.

SG

Bay Ridge?

I was just shocked. I mean, I don't think I knew anyone who lived all the way out there.

KEITH

Crazy, right? Didn't even know they made 'em this cool in Bay Ridge.

SG

Well, it was good to meet you, Frankie. Thanks for counting the cash.

I held my hand out for a pound.

DUNKS

Yeah, man, thanks for hanging out.

FRANKIE

No prob. I'll count money for you anytime.

KEITH

I bet you will.

Keith knocked him on the shoulder.

KEITH

Come on, kid. Before your mom chews me out.

Fives all around from Keith. A hug for Alexis.

Once me, Dunks, and Alexis got back to Union Square, we took a seat on the steps right where all the skateboarders and BMX kids practiced their tricks. Their girlfriends and groupies sat with their legs crossed at the ankles, watching as some crazy kid attempted to balance himself, standing on the seat of his bicycle. His homeboy was filming the whole thing, and the tattooed, blue-haired, pierced ear/cheek/chin/brow/neck punks—Dunks's people, definitely—cheered him on.

SG

So, just so I'm clear, you and Keith are in, right?

Dunks sat on one of the buckets he brought, and Alexis sat next to me on the steps, his long legs stretched out in front of him. Me and Dunks looked at him, but he didn't look at us. He just gazed at the balancing act.

ALEXIS

Depends. What's the plan?

SG

What do you mean?

ALEXIS

I mean, y'know, what y'all really wanna do? Y'all just playing for shits and giggles, or y'all playing for real?

DUNKS

What it look like we doin'?

Dunks came out of nowhere with a jolt of confidence. He spoke with attitude like he suddenly wasn't scared of this dude. Like he suddenly wasn't some weird, strange rich kid.

Alexis looked at him. His face, stone. No smile. No emotion. No way to read what he was thinking. He just glared at Dunks for long enough to shrink the nuts of any gangster. And Dunks just stared back, waiting for an answer.

Then Alexis broke, his face softening. He turned to me. Then back to Dunks. Then he looked straight ahead as the crowd screamed and moaned as the kid standing on the bike bit it.

ALEXIS

We're in. But my dream is to record in a major studio. So we use the money we make for making an album. I mean, what good is it to play shows when you can't leave your mark on history, knowhatimsayin'?

Dunks cheesed, then sucked his smile back in to keep up the whole tough act. I just nodded.

SG

I know exactly what you're saying.

I was pretending I wasn't hype. Making an album in one of these places that my heroes did was my dream. I mean, playing music was really my dream, but making an album—a real album to live forever—that's something different.

SG

But before we move forward—

DUNKS

For world domination.

SG

Right. Anyway, before we move forward, just to be clear so there's no weird confusion, what's the deal with you and Keith?

ALEXIS

What you mean?

SG

You know what I mean, man. What's the deal?

I was asking just because, I don't know, she was kinda cute. And even though I was totally against dating people you play with, especially after what happened to my mom and dad, I just needed to know if this guy was a boyfriend or just a bodyguard. Especially if we were going to be a band. Just gotta know where everybody stands.

ALEXIS

Ain't no deal, man. It's not like that with us. Keith is like my sister. She's been with me since day one. We play together, we laugh together, we even been arrested together.

SG

Arrested?

Not like I didn't know anybody who had been arrested. I just wasn't expecting him to say that.

ALEXIS

Yeah.

SG

For what?

Alexis rocked forward like an old man, struggling to stand. Once he made it up, he bent down and stretched to touch his toes. A guy that big probably has to stretch a lot. A whole lotta muscles that can cramp up, especially since everywhere has to be too small for you. Dunks and I looked up at him as if he was just another skyscraper.

ALEXIS

For taggin'.

SG

Taggin', as in graffiti?

ALEXIS

Yeah, man. Matter fact, we were right across the street.

He eased back down on the cement step.

ALEXIS

Remember that big music store right there, on the corner?

SG

Everybody knew that store. They had every single CD in the world.

ALEXIS

Well, we used to go in there all the time and just tag the covers of everybody's albums. We would just go through rows and rows of albums, inking them up. I guess it was like our way of visualizing ourselves there one day, y'know? Our music in that store.

Alexis looked across the street at what now is a bank.

ALEXIS

Stupid store ain't even there no more.

SG

Wait, so what was your tag?

Alexis reached behind him and grabbed his bass case. He pointed to silver bubble letters drawn across the side. DEFF.

DUNKS

DEFF? Like deaf?

ALEXIS

Man, you're brilliant.

DUNKS

No, you're brilliant!

Dunks's eyes were wide. He was not being sarcastic. At all.

ALEXIS

So one day, we were tagging the CDs, and I remember I was on an old Run-DMC album, and I was writing DEFF over DMC, and right when I wrote the D, I got a tap on my shoulder. Game over.

SG

But what did Keith do? Run?

A man came up to Dunks.

STREET GUY

Yo, man, you got a light?

He was holding half a cigarette and smelled like half a bottle of liquor. Dunks pulled a matchbook from his back pocket and handed it to the man.

Not sure why he had matches because, like I said before, Dunks doesn't smoke even though he looks like he does. He looks like he smokes everything.

ALEXIS

Naw, man, that ain't Keith's way. I gave her the signal to jet, but she just turned around and put her hands behind her back. The cop hadn't even gotten to her yet. He was busy cuffing me. And I wasn't gonna run. I'm too big. I make any moves, I'm a dead man, knowhatimsayin'?

SG

Right.

ALEXIS

But Keith just took it like a soldier, a real friend. We went down together. She held her chin up and let the cop slap the cuffs on her.

DUNKS

Y'all did time?

ALEXIS

Time? For taggin'?

Alexis laughed, and I could almost see *Where'd this guy come from?* floating around his brain.

ALEXIS

Naw, man. We got community service. Thirty days. I did mine at the firehouse, washing trucks and stuff like that. They put Keith in a hospital helping out the youth programs in the cancer ward. That's where she met Frankie.

SG

Frankie worked there too?

As soon as it left my lips, I knew it was a ridiculous question. Alexis was looking at me like I was a fool.

ALEXIS

No, man. Frankie's like thirteen. Keith hooked up with Frankie because he has cancer.

SG

What? Frankie? The kid who was just with us?

ALEXIS

Yeah. He's got this cancer called mesothelioma.

DUNKS

Yeah, I seen the commercials.

ALEXIS

Yeah, well, this is the real thing.

Alexis put his hands behind him and leaned back to rest his weight on his arms. I'm sure his back was starting to hurt.

ALEXIS

Keith met him her first day there. That's when they got into a conversation about music, and it was like all of a sudden she found her long-lost little brother. Like, he was one of us—a music head. At the time he had just started going through chemo and was sick all the time. Keith would come over with her horn and the mute, and play tunes for him. The kid's got a thing for jazz. Go figure.

DUNKS

Jazz?

Dunks stood up to stretch. He lifted his arms over his head, and his T-shirt, a size or two too small, lifted just enough to show his pale and strangely hairy belly.

DUNKS

It's not every day you can have a convo about jazz with anybody, let alone a little kid.

ALEXIS

Word. Tell me about it.

Alexis extended his legs out in front of him again.

ALEXIS

```
Then Frankie started losing his hair, and
in a matter of weeks, it was all gone.
```

SG

```
That's why he wears the hat.
```

Not like it's uncommon for boys to wear hats, but I still felt like I was piecing together some kind of puzzle.

ALEXIS

```
No, man, his hair's been grown back.
The kid just likes hats. And don't
worry, he's okay. The cancer has been in
partial remission for a while. He's doing
much, much better. But when he was going
through the treatment and lost his hair,
that's when Keith shaved hers.
```

Wow.

Wow. Wow. Wow.

When I first saw Keith, I knew there was something about this girl, blowing her horn, dazzling the crowd, her fingers pumping the valves, her cheeks sucking in and blowing out like Dizzy. It was obvious that musically, she was gifted, like some sort of time traveler. Like she was really from the twenties, used to playing in smoky juke joints, or from New Orleans, marching down the street with the rest of the brass band—just from somewhere else, another time. I know I sound like Dunks, but it's true. But now, hearing this story, about how she didn't bail on her homie, and how she took a kid under her wing to help him through a hard time, even shaving her head because of it—now I knew for sure she was amazing.

ALEXIS

```
Look.
```

Alexis pulled out his phone and flipped through picture after picture until he got to the one he wanted to show us.

ALEXIS

```
This is how she used to look.
```

It was Keith with long sandy brown hair. She was unreal.

DUNKS

```
Let me see.
```

Dunks stood behind Alexis as he held the phone up so Dunks could get a closer look.

DUNKS

```
Wow.
```

SG

```
Right.
```

ALEXIS

```
I know.
```

Alexis slipped the phone back into his pocket.

ALEXIS

```
Kinda crazy, right?
```

SG

```
But she still looks good, with the baldy.
```

Dunks didn't say nothing, even though I knew he felt the same way.

Alexis just looked at us both like we were talking about his sister. And in a way, we were.

ALEXIS

```
Come on, man!
```

CHAPTER 7

SO WE WERE A BAND. A REAL BAND. DRUMS, GUITAR, BASS, trumpet, and Frankie. Yes, Frankie was one of us, even though we didn't really know what exactly he was going to do yet. But it didn't matter. He was a bandmate.

Now, when you have a band, there are a lot of things that have to happen. Things that you have to do to make sure your band is legit.

Number 1. Gotta have a place to practice. I mean, we were obviously gonna be playing out in public, so we couldn't practice outside. How many bands practice at the arena? Not cool. So we had to have a place to jam, and for us, the easiest place for that to happen was Dunks's place, since he, well, had his own apartment.

The first time everybody came over, which was a few days after we had the jam—the takeover—in Union Square, we were all boosted about playing, but Keith, Alexis, and Frankie were super weirded out by Dunks's house.

KEITH

Dude, you never clean this place? Like,

I know y'all look at me like one of the guys, but damn.

DUNKS

It *is* clean.

And he wasn't lying. It was much cleaner than it usually was. I had helped Dunks straighten it up a little before they came over. Tossed out all the containers of old Spanish rice. Apparently it was a requirement to have Styrofoam bins of old food lying around in order to live in this building.

ALEXIS

If by clean, you mean filthy, then yes, it's spotless in here. You're Martha Stewart, bro!

He set his bass case on the floor and squatted down to open it up. I got the feeling he wasn't cool with sitting on the couch like Keith.

DUNKS

Yeah, yeah, yeah, but look at this setup.

Dunks waved his hand over all his musical equipment.

KEITH

Now *this* is clean.

Keith rocked up off the couch and walked over to the mix-up of wires and cords and screens and knobs. Frankie stood over it, staring at it all, like he was having some kind of religious experience. He held a small cup of vanilla ice cream that Keith had bought him, which I found out later was a ritual they started when he was in chemo (they said it helped with the pukey feeling).

Frankie spooned small bits of it into his mouth every few minutes.

DUNKS

Check it.

Dunks plugged in his guitar. He strummed a chord. Then he turned a few knobs as the chord rang out, going from a normal note to a weird synthesized pulse, almost like a siren.

DUNKS

See, this is what Pluto Music sounds like.

KEITH

Then my ass needs to stay right here on Earth.

Everyone laughed, and Dunks pretended to ignore us, tucking his chin down by his armpit so he could sneak a sniff.

Eventually, after everybody got out all their "Dunks is dirty" jokes, the rest of us got set up, plugged in, and ready to jam. I started it off with something simple, taking it easy on a bucket. Then Alexis came in, his bass rumbling through the room like thunder. Then came Dunks with a mean blues lick. The kid always knew what to do. Then came Keith with the horn, playing it low and mellow.

I looked over at Frankie. He leaned against the wall, bobbing his head, a slight grin smeared across his face, like he was watching the sun come up. Like he knew he was seeing something special happen. We all looked at each other, in Dunks's dirty-ass living room, all of us smirking, feeling the exact same way.

So that's where the practices were going to take place. On to the next thing.

Number 2. Practice schedule. This was easy to nail down, mainly because we weren't really "practicing." We were just jamming, but we knew what to do to rock out. It felt like it must have felt back in the day, when blues players in the South would just pop by and sit in with each other randomly, and knew exactly what to play.

Music is a language like any other language. When you understand it, you know how to respond—how to communicate. That's all this was. The four of us—five, counting Frankie—communicating. Talking shit.

So we decided to practice all the time. After Alexis and Keith were off work (Keith still worked at the hospital doing youth programs but was now getting paid for it), everybody would just come through Dunks's house. He'd treat us all to arroz con pollo and lime soda, and then we'd get busy.

Moving on. Number 3. Band name.

DUNKS

Okay, so I've been thinking about it. And I wanted to know what you guys thought about the Galactunes.

This was maybe two weeks after we had been practicing together as a band.

ALEXIS

Man, what?

Alexis looked at Dunks like he was crazy.

SG

`Man, what the hell are you talking about, dude?`

KEITH

`Galactune sounds like something old people have. Like, "Baby, I would come see y'all play, but my galactunes are all outta wack."`

SG

`You want us to sound like old people sickness? But seriously, Galactunes?` *`Galactunes?`*

DUNKS

`Well, do y'all have something better?`

Dunks poured soda into a mug that had "I DONT KNOW KARATE, BUT I KNOW KA-RAZY" in red on it. It also had James Brown's face on it.

Awesome.

Silence. Nobody said a word. None of us had a clue about what the band should be called, but one thing is for sure, we were *not* going to be the Galactunes. Not going to happen.

SG

`Let's just come back to it. It'll come when it comes.`

KEITH

`That sounds like a plan.`

DUNKS

```
Cool. But until it comes, we're the
Galactunes.
```

Number 4. The last thing we had to figure out was where we were actually going to play. This is when things got interesting. Now, at first, it seemed like this was a no-brainer. We would play where we'd started. At Union Square, on the steps, at nine. After weeks of prepping, acting crazy, and trying new things at Dunks's house, we decided to finally go hit the streets and see how people would respond to our new sound. Union Square was going to be our stage.

Every other night, Alexis, Keith, and Frankie would meet me and Dunks there. Alexis would always have his bass resting up on his belly as he tuned it. Keith sat on Alexis's bass case next to Frankie, fooling around with her horn. Dunks and I came and gave everybody dap, set everything else up, and before you know it—under streetlights, which for some reason at Union Square always seemed like concert lights—we were in full swing.

It always started with me. Whatever I played, the band took their cue from and followed up. The first session, or show, or whatever you wanna call it, I chose a Savion rhythm from *Bring in 'da Noise, Bring in 'da Funk* that turned into a nasty hip-hop groove that had everybody rocking.

The Union Square punks were sitting in a circle on their skateboards and BMX bikes freestyling, the breakers were breaking, and everybody else watched all stiff and awkward, tapping their feet like they were dying to jump out of their skin, but instead they just dropped money in Keith's case along with geeky vanilla smiles.

Every night was a good night. We'd make a couple bucks, which we'd use a little of to go and get pizza, and the rest I would keep to stash away. The plan was to save as much as possible to rent time in one of these places like The Record Factory or Electric Lady studios. A real studio. Not one of these "my homeboy got a mic in his closet" ones. Not that those were bad, but we weren't rappers. Having a mic in your closet does nothing for us because all of us can't fit in your closet. Hell, Alexis can't even fit in your closet.

I was like the band treasurer, mainly because I pretty much had to be. Keith and Alexis weren't comfortable walking through the projects with that kind of cash on them, which I totally understood, and they also weren't comfortable with Dunks keeping the money, in fear that he would lose it in the junkyard he called home. And Frankie was thirteen. No. So I kept it in a shoebox my uncle gave me and kept the box pushed way under the couch.

Anyway, we'd play Union Square every other night, and just as pizza was our after-show ritual, our preshow ritual was arguing about a band name.

From Galactunes, Dunks had suggested Space Rockers. No. Then Orbit Orchestra. Nope. Then Sonar. Not as bad as the others, but still, no.

DUNKS

`Aight, what about this one?`

Dunks was gearing up to announce his latest suggestion for a band name, strapping up his pink guitar on the steps of Union Square, when we felt the first raindrop. This was probably our tenth or eleventh time playing, and we had started to bring a lot of people out. Like, we had a few regulars who came every time, standing in the crowd ready to dance. We had also had this conversation ten or eleven times.

DUNKS

`What about Sonic Solar System?`

Alexis just shook his head. Keith kept blowing air through her horn.

DUNKS

```
And for short we could call ourselves
Triple S.
```

SG

```
Too close to Triple X.
```

The biggest raindrop in the world landed on my forehead.

DUNKS

```
S and X are far apart from each other.
That's not what I meant.
```

KEITH

```
S-S-S.
```

Keith gripped her horn like a handgun and pointed it at Dunks.

KEITH

```
Stupid, stupid, stupid.
```

Dunks looked sour from that one. Keith noticed and apologized right away.

KEITH

```
Let's just let it come, man.
```

She softened up, as the rain started to make itself more known. Believe it or not, over the few weeks we had been playing together, we had never had to deal with a washout. New York was having one of those hot and dry summers. So hot and so dry that there was no point in checking the weather because you knew it was going to be what it had been every day for the past two months . . . hot and dry.

But on this night maybe we should've, because it looked like the sky was going to open and pour right on us. We had equipment, instruments, and all kinds of doodads and knickknacks—mostly mine—to pack up, and the rain wasn't waiting. Within a matter of minutes, it had gone from a few drops, to a few more, to a sprinkle, to a drizzle. The crowd had started to scatter, and at that point it was clear that we weren't going to be able to play.

And then, out of nowhere, Frankie earned his spot in the band. As we all scrambled—me grabbing buckets, Dunks snatching cords from the amp, Alexis rushing to put his bass back in its case—Frankie came to Keith and suggested something genius.

FRANKIE

Yo, why don't we go underground?

KEITH

Let's go underground!

ALEXIS

Everyone, we're going underground!

And the band took off running toward the Union Square subway steps with, strangely, a ton of strangers—fans—running behind us.

CHAPTER 8

THAT RAINY NIGHT MIGHT'VE BEEN THE BEST MOMENT OF my life. And I had no idea it would be. Growing up in New York, you see the subway musicians and all that, but it's not really something you dream of being. No one's ever like, "When I grow up, I wanna bang on buckets in the subway." But that's exactly what happened. And what we found down there was pretty much our musical home.

First of all, and I never noticed this before, but the acoustics down there are incredible. Every clack of my drumsticks on a plate or a bucket or whatever, every booming pluck of Alexis's bass, every shriek of Dunks's guitar, every honk of Keith's horn—every everything sounded like we were playing in some kind of concert hall. And as we played, not only did our regulars come party with us, swiping their fare cards for admission to our show, but also the people coming down to take a train were held up, frozen by our groove, their trains whirring by over and over again.

I sat in the back on my crate, my arms flying all over the place, sweat dripping down my face, looking out at everyone.

It was like it was all happening in slow motion. Like we were all underwater. Big Alexis, his back to me, yanking at the strings of his bass, his body a giant pretzel knotting itself with every rumble. Keith, marching around with her horn to her mouth, her cheeks puffed out, one hand on her hip just to show off. Dunks, the alien string bean, his head tilted all the way back as if he was really communicating with someone or something out of this world. And Frankie, who stood with us, bounced his shoulders, and swayed to the music. Here we were, a band—still unnamed. But we didn't know at the time, that would only be for one more night.

I GOT HOME LATE. I think it was like one in the morning when Dunks and I came schlepping the pushcart with all our crap in it up the steps of the apartment. Once we got to our floor, we did our secret handshake.

I forgot to mention, we also made up a secret handshake that we all could do. It's kind of a big part of being in a band. Number 5. Gotta have a special shake—something that ties everybody together, that only we know. For us, it was slapping the backs of our hands together twice, then slapping our palms together three times, then sliding off the fingertips. It sounds corny, but if you see it, it's pretty damn slick.

Inside was pitch black. I could hear Uncle Lucky snoring loud from his room in the back of the apartment. I was exhausted and felt like I probably shouldn't even turn the light on, and instead just bumble to the couch and crash. Sticky, stinky clothes on and all. But I didn't. Because I had to put the money in the shoebox. I ran my hand along the wall, searching for the light switch.

With a click, the living room lit up, and I was met by a woman lying across my bed—the couch. My mother.

STUY'S MOM

Hi, baby.

Half her face was buried in the pillow, her eye flittering, trying to adjust to the light.

SG

`Ma? What are you doing here?`

She started to tear up.

STUY'S MOM

`Well, me and Dom, we . . . we, uh . . .`

She struggled to get it out, and all I could do was pray that she said "broke up."

STUY'S MOM

`We got into it.`

She lifted her face off the pillow. Her left eye looked more like a burnt biscuit. It was so swollen and so dark.

SG

`He hit you?`

I took a seat on the couch. I pulled the sticks from my back pocket and squeezed the wood as tight as I could.

SG

`That asshole put his hands on you?`

My eyes instantly filled up.

My mother wiped a tear away from her own face, then reached over to try and wipe a tear from mine, but I moved away.

STUY'S MOM

`It's okay, Stuy. Really.`

SG

Where's Uncle Lucky?

STUY'S MOM

Asleep.

SG

He ain't do nothing?

STUY'S MOM

He tried, but I begged him to stay here, to let it go. And that's what I'm gonna ask you to do too. I just wanna stay here for the night. Y'know, let things settle down a bit.

SG

What?

I couldn't believe what I was hearing. My mom. Even though we were beefing, she was still my mom.

SG

So you just gonna go back so he can do it again?

Then it dawned on me.

SG

Has he done this before?

My heart was pounding, and my breathing had started to get away from me, I was so mad.

STUY'S MOM

No.

I could tell she was lying. I just knew it. It was like our roles were suddenly reversed, and she was my kid and I was the parent. She repeated it, I guess to try to convince me that she was telling the truth.

I didn't know what to do. I squeezed the sticks harder and harder, until finally I just couldn't take it anymore, and I banged them up against the wall as hard as I could. I saw Dummy's face, his yelling mouth, his fists, and I gritted my teeth as I banged and banged. Over and over and over again.

My mother shrunk into a tight ball, wincing every time I slammed the sticks against the wall.

STUY'S MOM

Stop it, Stuy! Please stop!

I could hear her yelling, but I couldn't stop until finally Uncle Lucky came bursting into the living room. He wrapped his arms around me tight to restrain me and squeezed until I calmed down.

UNCLE LUCKY

Hey! I gotta live here!

When he saw that I wasn't stopping, that I was freaking out, he started to whisper:

UNCLE LUCKY

Okay, okay. That's enough. Calm down, nephew. Calm down.

He slowly eased up his grip, until finally letting go.

SG

```
What are we gonna do, Unc? What are we
gonna do?
```

I threw my drumsticks to the floor. My breathing was heavy, my face wet.

My uncle stepped back and sized me up. He took a deep breath. He shot his eyes at my mother, who sat on the couch with her hand over her mouth.

UNCLE LUCKY

```
Tonight . . . we're going to go to bed,
nephew.
```

SG

```
What?
```

UNCLE LUCKY

```
I know you're mad.
```

He swallowed what I guessed was his courage.

UNCLE LUCKY

```
I'm mad too. But see, your mom here, she
don't want us to do nothing.
```

STUY'S MOM

```
Just . . . just let this one go. Just
this one time. For me. Please.
```

I looked at her, then shook my head, totally disappointed. In her. In Lucky. He dropped his head and walked back to his room. Uncle Lucky slammed his door, which let me know that this was killing him too, but he really was going to try to respect my mom's wishes.

STUY'S MOM

```
Can you just come here?
```

She opened her arms. Her voice was low and still a little shaky, but there was no denying that motherly warmth. What was I supposed to do?

Even though I was still pissed—first about our original issue, about which was her choosing Dummy over me, and now over the fact that her first choice turned out to be a woman-beater, my mother another one of his victims—she was still my mom. And I had missed her. So I sat on the couch, and she wrapped her arms around me, and it was like that that we slept through the night.

She had already left by the time I woke up. And at first I was sad about it, just because we didn't get a chance to talk about the music and what I was doing with the band. And even though she was gone, the way I felt about the whole thing wasn't. I checked my cell phone. She had left me a text message.

i love you stuy. dont worry about me. im fine.

I didn't respond. I had nothing to say.

I opened my uncle's laptop and watched a few Savion Glover clips on YouTube to try to take my mind off things. Savion, back in the day on *Sesame Street*, which was funny. (He kinda looked like Keith, which was weird.) Savion on *Dancing with the Stars*, which was pretty cool. Then I got to Savion at the end of a movie called *Bamboozled*. I had never seen the movie, but judging from the five-minute clip, it was clear that he was pissed about something. And then he started to tap wildly. Violently. His feet slapped against the wooden floor loudly. Like gunshots.

I used my fingers and began tapping out the rhythm on the coffee table, listening closely to Savion's feet, and repeating the clip for about an hour straight, until I was banging the table with anger, causing my fingers to bruise and become sore.

That night, when we all met up at Dunks's, I was still in a funky mood. What can I say? Some things are just hard to shake.

DUNKS

```
What's wrong with you?
```

SG

```
What?
```

DUNKS

```
Something's wrong with you. I can tell.
```

Dunks was putting a megaphone in front of his amp to see what kind of effects he could get. I was just wondering why the hell he had a megaphone just lying around his house.

ALEXIS

```
Yeah, me too.
```

SG

```
Nothing. Just got a lot on my mind.
```

KEITH

```
Dude.
```

She didn't follow it up with anything. That was it. Just dude.

Dunks noodled around a little on his guitar, everything coming out staticky through the megaphone, almost like he was playing over a telephone, on speakerphone.

SG

Look, let's just pack up and head out. Back to Union Square, right?

KEITH

Underground.

SG

I think that's our best bet after last night.

ALEXIS

Hell yeah.

DUNKS

Yep.

Dunks unplugged his guitar. He bent down and picked up the megaphone. He put it to his mouth and pulled the trigger on it. Dunks spoke into the megaphone, sounding robotic and way too loud.

DUNKS

Frankie, you're a genius!

That's probably how he wished his voice sounded all the time.

WE CAUGHT THE TRAIN to Union Square instead of walking like we normally did, and it was while we were riding that I spilled the beans about my attitude and what had happened the night before.

SG

So last night I get home and my mother is there.

Of course the four of them looked at me, confused. I mean, Dunks knew the deal between me and my mom (and was just looking confused because he always looks confused), but Keith, Alexis, and Frankie didn't know the history.

SG

We're not really talking.

KEITH

Oh. Why not?

SG

Long story. But to make it short, she chose her boyfriend over me.

The train came to a screeching stop. The doors opened, and Alexis had to step off just so that he didn't block the door.

SUBWAY RECORDING

Stand clear of the closing doors, please.

People got off. People got on, then Alexis reappeared as the doors were closing. He leaned against the double doors with his bass case standing up in front of him. Keith took an empty seat next to an old Jewish guy with a big black hat and long curls dangling from each side of his face. Dunks sat across from her. Beside him was Frankie. On Frankie's other side was a guy who looked just like Dunks. Weird. It was like a Dunks sandwich. I stood between them all and held the pole.

ALEXIS

```
Ouch.
```

SG

```
Right.
```

I rubbed my hands together. They had become rough over the years, from the drumsticks. Then I gripped the pole again quickly as the train jerked.

SG

```
But last night, she showed up at my
uncle's crib with a black eye.
```

DUNKS

```
What?
```

SG

```
Yeah, man. Ol' boy smacking around on
my mom. And she talking 'bout "Don't do
nothing, Stuy. Let it go, Stuy." What the
hell kinda mess is that?
```

I could feel myself beginning to boil. My voice getting louder and louder.

Another stop. Alexis didn't move. He made people squeeze past him. His face was squished into a tight ball.

ALEXIS

```
So what you do?
```

SG

What you mean? What could I do? I had to just eat it.

KEITH

I dare some fool to try to pull that crap on me. He'll get this horn straight across his teeth.

I believed her, and judging from the Jewish guy's face when she said it, so did he.

SUBWAY RECORDING

This is Fourteenth Street, Union Square. Transfer is available for the 4, 5 . . .

FRANKIE

Y'all ready?

Frankie was getting us to focus on what we were about to do. He really was like a little manager. And it was good, because I really didn't want to talk any more about my mother and her drama. I just wanted to play. Get it out.

Our setup time had gotten pretty quick, and once we were off the train, it only took us about ten minutes before we were ready to play. Everybody took their places, and people rushed by us, running through the maze of underground tunnels like ants.

DUNKS

Okay, Stuy. It's on you.

Dunks faced me with the pink guitar dangling from his shoulder.

ALEXIS

Yeah, man. Take us where you want us to go, knowhatimsayin'?

Alexis hiked his bass up and got it comfortably up on his belly.

I sat on my crate for a second, the sticks in my hand. I thought I was ready to play, but I just couldn't think of anything.

Keith looked over at me. I just shrugged. She stepped closer.

KEITH

Just play whatever you think goes with the way you're feeling, man. Like, like a soundtrack for it all.

I looked at her, nodded, and began with the Savion Glover rhythm I had been practicing. The angry one from the end of that movie. I played hard, and for the first two or three measures, I played alone.

Dunks, Keith, Alexis, and Frankie all faced me, bobbing their heads. They watched as I worked this out, this messed-up feeling. Every hit was hard and raw, and the beat was enough to snap your head right off your shoulders. And I was in it.

All the way in it.

I looked up and simply said loud enough for them to hear me:

SG

This is the soundtrack.

All four of their eyes got big, and all at once we realized what our band name was. Keith grabbed Frankie and whispered in his ear. No one knew what she said, but while Alexis finally began to pluck his bass, slow and low, Frankie grabbed the random megaphone that Dunks brought just in case he wanted to slip into alien mode.

It was just me and Alexis, rocking a groove heavy enough to knock a train off the tracks. Frankie was standing in front of us all, fooling around with the megaphone. A crowd had started to gather.

Dunks looked a little confused, and I was too, but I didn't have time to worry because I was lost in the music.

All of a sudden, feedback came blaring through the megaphone. Then, the soft voice of a thirteen-year-old boy. Our little man, Frankie.

FRANKIE

`Everybody gather round!`

He looked back at Keith, who had just lifted her horn to her mouth. She winked at him and nodded.

FRANKIE

`Come grab hold of a brand-new sound!`

He paused to catch his breath, nervous, as the rhythm built up behind him. Then, in the most epic way possible:

FRANKIE

`We . . . are . . . Soundtrack!`

Yes. Yes we are.

CHAPTER 9

SG

What the hell? Where did that come from?

I LOOKED AT FRANKIE. THE SHOW WAS OVER, AND HE STOOD in front of me counting all the money. Dunks and Alexis were unplugging everything, wrapping cords around their arms, then slipping them off their elbows into neat circles.

KEITH

Been practicing it for a while when we catch the train home. The kid is one of us, so I figured we better give him a real job.

DUNKS

It was awesome, Frankie.

ALEXIS

Yeah. Now Dunks can give you his share of the money and feel like you actually earned it.

He put his big hand on top of Frankie's head and wiggled it around. Frankie broke loose and threw a jab. Of course, Alexis felt nothing.

FRANKIE

I've been practicing it. But we needed a name first, or it woulda been dumb.

SG

And now we got one.

KEITH

Thanks to me.

SG

What? I'm the one who said it to everyone.

KEITH

But I'm the one who said it to you, fool!

SG

True. So then it was both of us.

KEITH

Nope, just me.

ALEXIS

Doesn't matter, guys. What matters is . . . I'm hungry!

At the pizza shop, we talked about how many people were there to hear us play tonight. Frankie, of course, kept track of that.

FRANKIE

Tonight it was fifty-three. Yesterday it was forty-six. And last week, when we were outside every night—

He paused to check his phone, which is where he had been keeping track of the numbers.

FRANKIE

The highest day we had was thirty-three people.

SG

So the crowd is growing.

I brushed Parmesan cheese off the table.

DUNKS

Exactly, and this is just the beginning. We'll have all of Union Square packed within a month. Watch.

KEITH

That would be crazy. We'll see.

She put her crust on Alexis's plate as usual, then folded her plate into a tiny triangle before tossing it in the trash. She took a final slurp of her soda.

KEITH

You ready, Mr. Announcer?

Frankie stuffed what was left of his slice in his mouth. It was too much for him, and he did everything he could to keep sauce and cheese from oozing out. Stuff like that reminded us that he was definitely thirteen.

When they left, Dunks stepped outside to talk on the phone. One of his tenants. It was so easy to forget that Dunks was actually the landlord to a whole bunch of people, but whenever he got phone calls or text messages at random times from people complaining about how the roaches don't even wait until the lights are off before coming out anymore, and crazy stuff like that, I was reminded. He was more than just a music guy. He actually, strangely, had other real responsibilities, no matter how much it seemed like he didn't.

ALEXIS

So let me ask you something, Stuy.

Alexis munched on Keith's pizza crust as if it were a candy bar.

ALEXIS

Where your mother live?

SG

Bed-Stuy.

ALEXIS

No, I know that. I know she lives in Bed-Stuy.

Then he looked like he didn't want to ask me what he really wanted to know.

ALEXIS

I guess what I mean is, what's her address?

SG

```
Why you need her address?
```

Alexis looked straight ahead at the door, watching Dunks pace back and forth, waving his arms around like he was mad. I could only imagine what that conversation was about.

ALEXIS

```
Because she told you not to do anything
about that asshole, knowhatimsayin'? But
she didn't say that I couldn't.
```

I let the words enter my brain and sit there for a second before responding. I leaned in close and spoke just above a whisper:

SG

```
You gonna kill him?
```

ALEXIS

```
No!
```

Dunks swung the door open and started walking back over to the table. Alexis leaned in and lowered his voice before Dunks got to us.

ALEXIS

```
Do I look like a murderer, fool?
```

When he asked this, he gave me crazy eyes, and I wanted to say, "Yes . . . yes, you do look like a murderer." Instead I just scooted over a little. Alexis continued quickly before Dunks got to the table.

ALEXIS

I just wanna scare him.

DUNKS

What's going on?

I broke away from me and Alexis's conversation before answering Dunks, who looked like he had had enough. Of everything.

DUNKS

Ms. Dyson's bitchin' about her water pressure.

SG

It's too weak?

DUNKS

No. It's too hard for her. She's afraid that it's damaging her spine. Damaging her spine! So ridiculous. Last week she said the light in her apartment was too bright because of the light switches. I went up there and swapped out the bulbs for her to prove it's the watts in the bulb, not the switches on the wall.

SG

What you gonna do this time?

DUNKS

Nothing. Told her to try baths.

Dunks grabbed his pushcart and huffed.

DUNKS

`Y'all ready?`

Alexis started scooting out from the booth, glancing at me.

ALEXIS

`Text it to me.`

SG

`Okay.`

I wasn't really paying him no mind. But when I got home and I lay on the couch, the smell of my mother's hair still on my pillow, it all came back to me. I typed into the phone:

278 hancock btwn stuyvesant and malcolm x blvd

I waited for Alexis to text back. But he never did.

One thing I forgot to mention (though I'm sure you've noticed by now) is that I was the only one of us that didn't have a job. Alexis worked at a printshop, Keith worked for the hospital, and Dunks was a landlord. I was a bum, and Uncle Lucky wasn't paying me no money to clean up once a week. That was actually more like me paying him for letting me crash.

So, not long after that last call from Ms. Dyson, Dunks hired me as the super, mainly because he hated dealing with the people in the building and all their problems. When I say he hated, I mean he really hated. Whenever somebody would call or leave a note on his door about some gripe or problem they were having, Dunks would get so annoyed that his face went red. It was the only time that I really saw him upset.

So he brought me on to do his dirty work. Plus he figured I could use the money anyway.

As the super of the building, my days were filled with, pretty much, building chores. Somebody always needed something. Mr. Garcia up in 4A for some reason always, always, always flushed paper down the toilet. His deal was, he was a writer—maybe the craziest writer of all time. But he's an older guy, so he actually wrote, like, on paper. So whenever he messed up, or wrote something that he didn't like, he would rip the paper off the tablet, ball it up, and throw it on the floor. Y'know, like in old movies. At the end of the day—this is what he told me—he would look around and see all the scraps of paper, and freak out because he could physically see all his screwups lying all over the floor. But instead of trashing them, he would throw the paper balls in the toilet. He was too scared of throwing them away, because he thought someone would discover them and see how bad he was at writing. Either that, or they'd steal some of his ideas.

Dunks said Mr. Garcia used to burn them, but he was having too many close calls almost torching the whole damn building down. So now the old man tries to flush them. I swear, this dude's apartment flooded at least once a week. So there was that.

And then there was the Bednicks, who lived on the ground floor. Apartment 1B. Ms. Bednick was so sweet, but her son, Jamar, was a wild dude. He was one of these guys who fell in love with every woman that he met, but the chicks he happened to like were all crazy.

It's like he had the worst luck in the world when it came to the ladies.

So once a month, I had to go down there and have their apartment windows replaced because some nutso had thrown a brick through it, with some shaky-handed love letter attached. Jamar always showed them to me, almost like they were trophies or something. And the only reason Dunks hadn't booted them out of here is because Ms. Bednick paid extra every month to compensate for the craziness.

And then there was Ms. Dyson. Ms. Dyson, Ms. Dyson, Ms. Dyson. The oldest lady in the building, who seemed to always have a problem with something that usually had nothing to do with the building. It got to the point that Dunks stopped waiting for her to call and just told me to go check on her a few times a week. That way, he didn't have to deal with her calling him complaining all the time.

Apartment 3F. I rung her bell.

MS. DYSON

Who is it?

Her voice sounded like she smoked a pack a day, and that's exactly what she did.

SG

It's Stuyvesant, Ms. Dyson. Came by to see if you needed anything.

MS. DYSON

Oh, okay.

The unlocking process, clicks and clacks, then click-clack. The door opened, and cigarette smoke came rushing out as if even it was trying to get away from her.

MS. DYSON

I'm glad you're here. Thought you'd never come.

She stood there in pink pants and a soft blue button-up. She was so cute, but not cute enough to cover up her crazy.

SG

I was just here two days ago, ma'am.

MS. DYSON

Yeah, and the whole damn place started falling down around me right after you left.

Her apartment was weird, and I hated going to it because she was one of those people who saved everything. What you call them? Hoarders? Yeah, she was one of them. This lady must've had every single newspaper ever made. They lined the walls in stacks from floor to almost ceiling. I don't even know how she got them stacked that high. And in front of them were old issues of *Ebony* and *Jet* magazines. Like, thousands of them. It was cool and gross at the same time.

She grabbed me by the arm and walked me into her kitchen.

MS. DYSON

This.

She pointed to the refrigerator.

SG

The fridge?

MS. DYSON

Yeah.

SG

What about it?

MS. DYSON

```
It's broken.
```

I opened the door and put my hand inside. It was cool.

SG

```
No, it's not, Ms. Dyson.
```

MS. DYSON

```
Then why my food ain't getting cold,
then? Why is stuff melting, smarty?
```

Her head was cocked to the side like I was some dummy. I looked inside to try and find the temperature knob thing.

SG

```
Because of this thing. It's on two.
Should at least be on seven.
```

Ms. Dyson squeezed her little self in front of me so she could see. She smelled like mothballs. Or mold. I couldn't tell which one.

MS. DYSON

```
Well, how'd it get there?
```

SG

```
I don't know, but I'm guessing you
may have accidentally hit it. But now
everything should be fine, okay?
```

I turned it back up. She backed away from the fridge. And I backed away from everything until I was on the outside of her apartment.

Then, the locking process. The click-clack first, then clicks and clacks. Through the door, I said:

SG

```
See you in a few days.
```

Nothing.

After supering all day, I would come back to Uncle Lucky's, take a quick shower, then head over to Dunks's, where we would jam a little or watch internet clips, while he did things like paint his thumbnails black or draw weird designs on the back of his guitar.

I loved to watch old clips of musicians, like Hendrix (who Dunks loved, of course) or B. B. King, or old Run-DMC clips when the drumbeat was simple and crisp. If not that, I was checking for Savion. And when Dunks wanted to watch a clip, it was usually something about space travel, or advertisements about some new company that's planning to take people to space for like a million dollars or something.

Please. Ain't no way I'm paying somebody that much to send me up into the stars for a few hours. What if something happened and I got stuck up there with a bunch of aliens like Dunks? Nope. Not me.

We did this until everyone else came, which was always around six o'clock, because that was when Alexis got off work at the printing store. From there we'd order a quick bite from the Spanish spot, then head out to Union Square, for what over a few weeks was becoming our daily concert. And by concert, I mean, it was really becoming like a concert.

We would get there around eight and people would already be there, some patiently sitting on the floor, legs crossed, eating some snack they got from the subway concessions/magazine stand. Others standing talking to each other. And when Frankie weaseled through the crowd, creating a lane for us to walk through with all our equipment, the crowd would start clapping, just because we were there. This is before we even began! As a matter of fact, this is before we even unpacked our instruments! Clapping! For us!

I remember one of the craziest times at Union Square. I think we had been rocking for about a month at this point, and when we showed up, there was a line to get down the steps from the street to the subway station if you were trying to get in through the Fourth Street entrance, by what used to be the big record store.

I'll never forget that night, because it was another one of those times that changed everything, mainly because it was the first time that things didn't go smoothly.

It was the biggest crowd we had ever seen down there, everyone waiting for us to get going, but we were a man short. Alexis hadn't shown up. He texted me and said that he would meet us at Union Square, like usual, but when we got there, no Alexis.

We set up and went through our usual ritual of tuning up, spit blowing, and all that. Frankie had grabbed his megaphone, which had become like his best friend, and started warming up the crowd with a roll call.

FRANKIE

Is Brooklyn underground?

His voice burst through the megaphone. People would squeal and hoot, representing their borough or their neighborhood. Meanwhile, we were stalling, waiting for Alexis.

Finally, he showed up, looking crazy, like he had just rolled out of bed.

KEITH

You okay?

He didn't answer. He just hurried up, got his bass out, plugged it in, and gave everyone a nervous nod to let us know that we could finally start.

Frankie time.

FRANKIE

`Everybody gather round! Come grab hold of a brand-new sound!`

He was no longer nervous like he was the first time. Now he had become a pro. He held one hand up, and the whole crowd joined him in shouting:

FRANKIE AND CROWD

`We . . . are . . . Soundtrack!`

I put it right into a Clyde Stubblefield beat. Clyde Stubblefield was James Brown's drummer, so it's pretty much safe to say that dude was the funkiest drummer to ever walk the earth. And for some reason, that night I was feeling funky. And as soon as I started hitting, the band knew exactly what to do. Keith was doing nasty funk stabs on her horn. Dunks was doing funk licks, his hand strumming and muting, strumming and muting. And Frankie and his megaphone were egging the crowd on with random ad-libs like:

FRANKIE

`Ain't it funky now?! Union Square, can you feel it down in your bones?`

The crowd loved this kid. And he loved them.

The only issue was Alexis. He wasn't bringing it like he usually did. He wasn't spanking the bass like the funk called for. I mean, don't get me wrong, he didn't play bad, and judging from the way the crowd was sweating it out, nobody could even tell he wasn't really playing. But we could.

As soon as we wrapped the jam, Keith darted straight over to Alexis.

KEITH

What the hell? What was that?

She pulled the mouthpiece from her horn. Me and Dunks were also waiting for an explanation, while Frankie dug into the pile of money in Keith's trumpet case.

ALEXIS

My hand is acting up.

Alexis stretched his fingers out, then balled his hand back into a fist. He repeated this, and on the third or fourth time I noticed the bruises on his knuckles.

KEITH

Let me see it.

Keith reached for his hand. Alexis snatched it back.

ALEXIS

No! It's fine.

He turned around and started fiddling with his cord. I looked at Keith. She looked at Dunks, who stood bone straight. Frankie was still squatting, now counting the money. Keith squinted her eyes and glared at Alexis's back.

KEITH

Dude, why were you late?

Alexis stopped doing whatever he was doing, which we all knew was just avoiding us.

ALEXIS

Yo, Keith, when you become my mother?

Keith just glared at him, ice cold. Dunks and I just stood there watching as if we were witnessing the second coming of the David and Goliath showdown. And, of course, David won again, but not with rock and sling, but with freckles and eyes.

ALEXIS

Look, I just had to take care of something.

Now, when he said this, he glanced at me, and in that split second, I knew what had happened.

ALEXIS

It's taken care of now, and I won't be late again.

DUNKS

Sounds good to me. Can we go now?

Dunks started throwing everything in the pushcart.

DUNKS

Frankie, what we got?

No answer.

DUNKS

Frankie?

Frankie wasn't concerned about the band drama at all. He was too busy talking to a tourist. A young girl who didn't speak English, so I guess Frankie wasn't really talking to her, but they were definitely communicating. She wanted an autograph. From him. And of course, he gave it to her, along with a hug and a kiss on the cheek.

FRANKIE

Sorry. She said she heard the sound coming from underground and begged her folks to bring her to see it—to see us.

Then he got cocky.

FRANKIE

Well, really, to see me.

The nerve . . . From then on, we called him Famous Frankie.

On the way to get pizza, I walked next to Alexis, who hung back a little to let Dunks, Keith, and Frankie walk ahead of us. Dunks had a tape recorder in his hand, and held his arm out in traffic as if he were trying to catch a cab, when really he was just trying to tape the sound of cars whooshing by. It was his newest experiment in crazy . . . I mean, Pluto Music.

SG

Can I take a guess at what happened to your hand?

ALEXIS

```
Go for it.
```

SG

```
278 Hancock?
```

A police car came zooming down the street, the red and blue lights strobing, the siren screaming.

Alexis got a little tense. Like, I could see him shrink, just an inch, as the car sped by. He tried not to look nervous when he looked at me.

ALEXIS

```
Between Stuyvesant and Malcolm X Boulevard.
```

I knew it.

SG

```
Jesus, man.
```

I said it too loud. Frankie turned around to see what we were talking about. I lowered my voice. I wasn't even sure why this whole thing was a secret, but because Alexis seemed like he didn't want people to know that he was going to pretend to be one of my goons, I kept it on the hush.

SG

```
I thought you said we were going to
scare him?
```

ALEXIS

```
That was the plan, man. I swear. But the
dude got scrappy on me.
```

Sounds about right. Dummy is such a dummy.

SG

How bad did it get?

Alexis and I stopped at a corner. Dunks, Frankie, and Keith made the light and were already walking into the pizza shop.

ALEXIS

Bad enough.

Alexis took a step back so that the woman next to us could actually have a shot at hailing a cab. A cabbie wouldn't even be able to see her with Alexis standing in front of her.

ALEXIS

I went just to tell him to leave your mom alone, knowhatimsayin'? But when I got there and went into my whole thing, he started flipping on me.

The light changed.

ALEXIS

Next thing I know, he swung. And that was it. I just went into reflex mode. Now him and your mother are twins.

He looked at me with one eye closed.

ALEXIS

And I can guarantee his hurt a lot worse than hers.

I can't lie—even though that wasn't the plan at all, it made me feel a little better that Alexis made Dummy pay. Alexis closed his eye up. Wish he could've closed his life up. I know that sounds bad, but it's honestly the way I felt.

As Alexis held the pizza shop door open for me, I asked him:

SG

Was she there? My mother?

He walked up to the counter. Keith and Dunks and Frankie were already sitting, huddled around Dunks's tape recorder, listening to traffic sounds. We could hear that same cop car that passed us on our way to the pizza shop on the recording.

ALEXIS

Yeah.

SG

Shit.

ALEXIS

Hey, man, look at it this way, at least she knows it wasn't you who did it. Could've been anybody.

Alexis made a good point, but still, I was worried.

SG

She's my mother, man. Mothers always know.

Especially mothers who talk to their big brothers. My uncle Lucky talked to my mom all the time, keeping her updated on what was happening with me, the band and all that. I knew there was a good chance that my mother would be smart enough to put two and two together. And dumb enough to be mad.

And of course, I was right. The night only got more complicated when the text messages started coming through from my uncle and my mom as soon as we sat at the table with the rest of the band.

UNCLE LUCKY

wtf stuy! i dont feel bad about it but i hope this asshole doesnt try to do no punk shit like press charges on your friend

what was i supposed to do?
he wasn't supposed to hit him!
but something had to happen unc.

plus how would she even know it had anything to do with me?

STUY'S MOM

i asked you to leave it alone! i told you to let it go! why couldnt you just listen to me and mind your business?!

Like I said, smart . . . and dumb.

A horn honked. Not in real life, but on the recording.

I responded to my mother.

i dont kno what u talkn abt

STUY'S MOM

you better tell your friend to watch himself. dom is filing a report right now.

dont know what u talking bout. busy. ttyl

UNCLE LUCKY

i understand.

STUY'S MOM

you just dont understand.

KEITH

What I can't understand is why you two fools not eating.

I looked up from my phone after what seemed like forever. I hadn't touched my pizza. I glanced at Alexis. He hadn't touched his either.

KEITH

Hot box over here is texting his fingers off, and Edward Broke-hands over here is just pouting like he lost his best friend.

She reached over and pushed Alexis's plate closer to him.

KEITH

But I'm still here.

He forced a tiny smile. I couldn't even muster that up. Keith realized that something was really wrong.

KEITH

Okay. What's going on?

ALEXIS

Nothing.

I snapped my neck at him, surprised at the fact that he really was going to keep this thing a secret.

SG

Tell them, man.

ALEXIS

What?

SG

Tell them. We have to.

ALEXIS

No, we don't.

SG

Yes, we do.

I slid my phone, with my mom's text message open, to the middle of the table. Keith reached for it, but Alexis grabbed it first.

SG

He's pressing charges.

KEITH

Who?

Dunks took the recorder off the table, and Frankie nibbled on a pepperoni.

SG

My mother's boyfriend.

Alexis put the phone back on the table and bit down on his bottom lip. The big guy looked worried.

Keith looked at Alexis, her brother, her best friend. She leaned back against the booth cushion and dropped her head. It was like she already knew the story without us having to tell it. But Dunks was totally out of the loop, so it still had to be told.

ALEXIS

Okay, look, remember when Stuy told us about his mom's boyfriend hitting her?

Dunks nodded yes. Frankie nodded yes. Keith just slouched down in the booth and crossed her arms across her chest.

ALEXIS

Well, I offered Stuy my services. Just to scare that asshole, knowhatimsayin'?

SG

Right. The plan was just to scare him, so that he wouldn't do it again.

ALEXIS

Right. So I go over to Stuy's place, wait for somebody to come out so that I can slip in without hitting nobody's buzzer or anything. Knocked on the door. He opens it.

KEITH

Wait, how did you even know it was him?

ALEXIS

Lucky guess. I mean, there was a woman

standing behind him who looked just like Stuy.

Frankie started giggling.

SG

It's true. I look just like my mom.

ALEXIS

Yeah, so I made a safe bet. It happened so fast. I yanked his ass up by his shirt collar, yanking him out of the apartment and slamming him against the wall. What I had originally planned was to whisper in his ear something like, "I'll bite your fingers off if you lay another one on her."

SG

Wait, what?

I was shocked. It never crossed my mind that the scare tactic would involve eating body parts.

KEITH

What the hell, Alexis?

ALEXIS

Look. I thought it would work. And I thought it would be funny. But I didn't even get to say it, because as soon as I grabbed him, he just snapped on me and started fighting back.

DUNKS

Did he hit you?

Dunks returned to his open-mouthed, stuck position. He was so into the story that it looked like he could drool on the table at any second.

ALEXIS

Yeah. And that's when my reflexes kicked in, and I gave him a mean one—closed his eye right up. Hell, might have crushed that whole side of his face, for real.

Alexis put his messed-up right hand on the table. The knuckles were all swollen like big marbles under the skin.

KEITH

Shit. And he's pressing charges?

SG

That's what the text message says.

I leaned back and put my hands behind my head. I looked over at Alexis, who definitely looked worried. Though he was huge, when he was scared his face looked like he was a little boy.

SG

And it won't be hard for the cops to track him down, because my mom knows where we play every night, thanks to my uncle.

KEITH

Would she rat us out, though?

SG

Honestly, the way things are right now, I wouldn't even be surprised.

DUNKS

So what now?

We all sat around the table thinking, and then Frankie spoke up with perfect timing again, with another brilliant, genius, "this little kid might be the second coming of the Savior" idea.

FRANKIE

Why don't we just go on tour?

CHAPTER 10

LET ME CLARIFY. WHEN FRANKIE SAID "WHY DON'T WE JUST go on tour?" he didn't mean get a tour bus, travel around from venue to venue, where our roadies would set everything up for us, and there would be SOUNDTRACK in big letters and even bigger lights flashing across a big marquee. He didn't mean green rooms, where we had stupid special requests like "only yellow Skittles" or arroz con pollo made by the same guy we go to in the Lower East Side, but we'd be in China.

No, Frankie wasn't talking about us onstage with screaming groupies in the crowd, or us having to sign hundreds of autographs for them afterward. Nope. What Frankie meant by "Why don't we just go on tour?" was . . . run.

And that's what we did. Not in the sense of breaking out and sprinting away from cops. But in the sense of, our days at Union Square were over.

We all hung out at Dunks's the next night and talked about what our next steps were and, more importantly, what the next stop was, especially since we knew cops would probably be looking for Alexis. Everybody threw out their suggestions.

DUNKS

Brooklyn.

KEITH

Not Brooklyn. That's too close to the scene of the crime. What about Dumbo? Down by the water.

SG

That's still Brooklyn. Plus it's too bougie. They walk around there whispering to each other. I'm sure they don't want our loud asses waking up their little dogs.

KEITH

Word. That's probably why I don't even look at it as really Brooklyn.

ALEXIS

I'll be arrested in no time over there.

His face instantly snapped back to worry.

FRANKIE

The Bronx.

EVERYONE

No.

No.

Hell no.

FRANKIE

Dang, I'm just saying it's far enough away. Nobody will know we're there.

SG

Exactly. So Famous Frankie won't be so famous.

Frankie saw where we were coming from.

FRANKIE

Oh. Bad idea.

Alexis sat on the couch with his bass on his lap. He rubbed his hands over the body like stroking the face of some girl he was in love with. It was weird to see a guy so big and so scary (sometimes) be so gentle and so sensitive with his instrument. At least whenever he wasn't beating the hell out of it when he was playing. When he wasn't rocking out, he protected that thing like he did Keith. Like he meant to do for me and my mom.

I got up off my milk crate to stretch my legs.

SG

I got an idea. Why don't we just hit the A train?

KEITH

On the train?

SG

No, not on the train. Just along the A line.

I leaned against the wall in front of a poster of Slash from Guns N' Roses. The top hat. The curly hair. The sunglasses. The guitar.

SG

```
Just hear me out. We start at West Fourth
Street station, then we hit Fourteenth
Street, then boogie up to Thirty-Fourth
and catch all the tourists and travelers.
```

I could tell Keith, Dunks, Frankie, and Alexis could see what I was saying.

SG

```
And then we crush Times Square.
```

KEITH

```
Hell yeah.
```

DUNKS

```
Boom! Then we'll have enough money to
cut a real album.
```

FRANKIE

```
And we can keep Alexis from getting
arrested.
```

Alexis just sat there nodding, pressing his fingers gently along the neck of his guitar almost as if he were pressing the keys of a piano.

ALEXIS

```
I appreciate all this, guys, but
I can't run forever, knowhatimsayin'?
```

Killed the whole vibe. All the enthusiasm was zapped right out of me, Frankie, Dunks, and Keith instantly.

SG

```
But this gives us time.
```

ALEXIS

```
Time for what?
```

SG

```
Time for me to get my uncle to convince
my mother to convince Dummy to drop the
charges.
```

ALEXIS

```
You think this dude, who, by the way,
might be blind in one eye now, is going
to drop the charges?
```

The truth is, no, I didn't think so. But still, it was worth a shot.

SG

```
I mean . . . he might. It's worth trying.
```

The one thing that I'm glad we didn't do when we first got together was start all that social media stuff for the band. (It was definitely next on the to-do list.) Like, we didn't have a social media page or anything like that, so all the hype that was building around us was happening the old-school way—word of mouth. This was a big deal now, especially since we didn't want to be traced or tracked by the cops. All they would've had to do was look online to see where we were playing and just show up, waiting for us as if they were some opening act or something.

But because we didn't have any of that, we had a better shot of getting away with bouncing around to hide our boy.

First stop, West Fourth Street station.

Here's what you need to know about the West Fourth Street station. It's the most, uh, colorful station of them all. Whatever happens aboveground happens underground, and aboveground are all the folks that a guy like Dunks would want in our first music video (if that ever happens). You know, weirdos and freaks. The Union Square crew times a thousand. Dudes who wear tiny leather shorts and fishnet stockings on their legs and arms. Guys in gowns and high heels, walking better than I bet Keith could walk in them. Ladies with tattoos of big hearts—hearts like the ones that beat, not like the "I love you" hearts—on their chests, and big chunky sneakers making them a foot taller than they really were.

So this is who we played for. Underground humans that I knew were humans, but that looked like aliens. And it was awesome. A trip, but awesome.

SG

Aight, Dunks. I think it's a good idea if you lead this one.

I slid the baking pan closer to me, our usual setup just about complete.

ALEXIS

Yeah, man. We're following you.

Keith stood to the side, staring down the platform.

ALEXIS

Yo, you ready?

Keith didn't respond. She was just stuck, staring like she saw Louis Armstrong's ghost standing at the end.

ALEXIS

Keith!

KEITH

My bad. It's just rats crawling around up here.

ALEXIS

Don't worry about 'em. Dunks is leading tonight, so they'll run off the platform in about two minutes.

There wasn't much of a crowd at first. Our guess was everybody was at Union Square, probably looking for us and wondering why cops were also snooping around doing the same thing. At West Fourth, there was a few people down there, but they were just waiting for the A train. Nobody knew who we were. Nobody cared.

Dunks held the pink guitar like a machine gun.

DUNKS

Famous Frankie. Do your thing.

He didn't like the way that sounded, so he repeated himself to try to sound more cool.

DUNKS

Thang. I mean thang. Do your thang.

Didn't work.

Frankie grabbed the megaphone and hit the button a few times, causing a screeching feedback. Then he put it to his mouth.

FRANKIE

```
Everybody gather round! Come grab hold
of a brand-new sound!
```

And all together—just the five of us now:

EVERYBODY

```
We! Are! Soundtrack!
```

Dunks let loose. I mean, it was like he just started on a thousand. No buildup. No warning. Just straight solo craziness, which usually was never a good idea. It's like you use up all your magic too quick that way. But he had already jumped in, so there was nothing the rest of us could do but trust him and let him rip.

After about thirty seconds of complicated guitar wailing, and Dunks bending and squatting and kicking like a wild man, the people on the platform started gathering, inching over like ninjas sneaking up on us. It's always funny to see it, because everybody always tries to act like they don't care. They pretend to just mind their business, like they don't hear the music. And nobody ever wants to give money, so they feel weird about coming to listen for free. Our job is to rock the money right out of their pockets and make them mind *our* business.

Dunks went into a nasty guitar lick and kept it going on and on.

Frankie took the megaphone and put it in front of the speaker the way we had seen Dunks do it in his apartment a while back.

The sound was insane. Loud and harsh and strangely dope. Dunks threw his head back and lost his mind, and just like that, the floodgates (or the star gates) were open, and the people started coming quick.

Now, I don't know if there was just people coming for the music because they heard it bursting through the concrete up there, or if there just happened to be a lot of people coming to catch the train all at the same time, but either way, once they saw and heard what was happening, they were hooked.

And this is before the rest of us even played a note. It was like Dunks was sending out a signal to the other aliens of New York and they were coming down five at a time, covered in tattoos and weird clothes.

A man wearing yellow girl drawls and a black scarf around his neck danced like he was under a spell, flinging his scarf back and forth like he was one of those ballerinas with the ribbons. It was nuts.

And after about five long minutes of Dunks just going ballistic, the rest of us joined in. Game . . . over.

About an hour later as we wrapped it up, unplugging and breaking down, I asked Frankie:

SG

What was the count?

FRANKIE

I got thirty-one.

Thirty-one people for the first show at West Fourth was pretty good.

KEITH

Guys, check this out. This lady . . .
What's your name?

DYLAN

Dylan.

KEITH

Dylan. She's been following us in Union Square.

SG

Word.

Frankie—Famous Frankie—ran over to shake her hand. Keith pushed him out of the way playfully.

ALEXIS

How'd you know we were here?

Alexis tried his best to hide the worry in his voice. Dunks walked over, biting at the calluses on his fingertips.

DYLAN

I didn't. Me and my friends went to Union Square yesterday to try to catch you guys, but you weren't there. Thought y'all were done. Tonight, I just ended up over here to grab food. Papaya Dog, right there.

ALEXIS

Yeah.

DYLAN

And here y'all are!

She shook her head like she couldn't believe we were standing in front of her. It was the first time I ever felt famous.

SG

How often did you come see us at Union Square?

DYLAN

As much as I could. Almost every night. I would try to come with different friends, y'know? And everybody would leave saying the same thing, that you guys are *amazing*. The songs are just insane.

DUNKS

They're really just jams. Not really songs. Just, I don't know, us working out stuff. If that makes sense.

DYLAN

It does. It does. And I'm gonna do my best to keep watching y'all work whatever it is out. As long as I can find y'all.

And that's when it hit me. She was the link, the missing piece to how we could stay low-key but still build this thing.

SG

Dylan, can I buy you a slice of pizza?

We couldn't go to our usual pizza spot for obvious reasons and instead had to settle for the most mediocre pizza ever. But I always hear musicians talk about eating crappy food whenever they're on tour, so I guess that made sense.

We squeezed into an uncomfortable booth in the corner and tried to choke down the slices, all while making small talk about what Dylan was studying in school.

DYLAN

Family studies.

SG

Word? You should use mine as research.

DUNKS

Or mine.

Dunks was the only one of us who had no problem scarfing his pizza down. It was like it was the first time he had eaten in a week. All that rocking out must've made him pretty hungry.

SG

Okay, Dylan. Here's the deal.

I wiped my mouth. I know the rest of the band was wondering what I had up my sleeve, and I was happy that they just trusted me and went with it, especially since I had invited her to our after-show ritual, which, even though it was never said, I knew was a big no-no.

SG

You know how every band has a street team?

Dylan chewed, and chewed, and chewed, and still had to take a sip of her soda to get the pizza down.

DYLAN

```
Uh huh.
```

SG

```
Well, we need somebody to do that for
us, but not in that corny way most
people do. You know, like flyers and all
that—naw. That's not what we're doing.
That's not really our way.
```

DYLAN

```
Okay.
```

She waited for me to get at whatever it was I was getting at. I could tell the rest of the band was waiting for the same thing.

SG

```
What we would need you to do is at our
shows, while we're up there playing, to
tell people where our next stop is.
```

DYLAN

```
Oh. Just let people know where you guys
are playing next?
```

SG

```
Yep.
```

I fanned a fly away from my food. Should've let the little guy have some. Maybe he would've enjoyed it more than me.

SG

```
But there's one catch.
```

Dylan looked at me, waiting for the bomb to drop.

SG

```
It's a secret. We're a secret. This whole
thing is a secret. So you literally have
to whisper it in people's ears.
```

I glanced around the table at everyone else. Keith flashed a smile, and so did Dunks and Frankie. Alexis just nodded.

DYLAN

```
It's like an underground movement. I
totally get it.
```

KEITH

```
Exactly. We'll tell you, and you secretly
tell other people.
```

DUNKS

```
It's brilliant.
```

ALEXIS

```
Yeah. It really is.
```

What's better than being brilliant is that the idea actually worked.

We played two more shows at West Fourth Street. The first one was good, but the second one, we absolutely killed. The whole set, we played this weird sixties pop-rock stuff. Like the Beatles. The ghetto Beatles. Keith joked that we were the Roaches.

KEITH

```
Roaches are just more edgy, y'know, more
```

gangsta than beetles are. Beetles don't even do nothing. But roaches scare the hell outta you, no matter who you are.

She put some lip stuff on.

ALEXIS

And they don't die. They just adapt.

KEITH

Exactly.

SG

Exactly.

People danced and clapped as Dunks played some psychedelic bubble-gum rhythm, and Frankie shimmied around giving the crowd a modern-day version of the Twist before having to stop and catch his breath.

By the end of it, we were tired and soaking wet, but that was okay because we were looking out at the most people we had ever seen at one of our shows. It looked like a hundred people, but Frankie let us know later that it was only fifty-four. Still, that's a lot.

Before the show, I pulled Dylan—who of course was there—to the side and whispered in her ear:

SG

Tomorrow, Fourteenth Street.

That's all I said. She nodded, and as the crowd grew and the party went to full tilt, we could see Dylan maneuvering slickly through the mob, whispering in random strangers' ears.

Especially the people who looked like they were really having a good time.

And the next day, as we came marching up the steps from the train onto the platform tunnel at Fourteenth Street, there was a crowd already waiting for us.

CHAPTER 11

THIS IS FOURTEENTH STREET. TRANSFER . . .

Fourteenth Street was the best station we played in. It was one of the cleanest ones, that's for sure. And they had these cool sculptures of alligators climbing out of sewers and all that. Just a dope place to play. Also, it's wide open, just one straight tunnel from the Fourteenth Street exit to the Sixteenth Street exit, with nothing blocking it except for a few pillars. So the sound was incredible.

That night was wild. To get off the train, come up the steps, and have people just start clapping for you is pretty crazy. And Frankie walked through the crowd with his hand in the air, like the star that he was. And even though Frankie was definitely soaking it all up, Keith was more into it than even he was. She was really gassed about it all. Her smile was so wide that it looked like it hurt. Imagine a smile so big that it causes you to have a migraine or something. That's how Keith's looked. On some clown shit.

We decided to set up in the middle, which is usually quick and easy, but the fact that the crowd was just sitting there watching us threw us off a little. But Famous Frankie kept them distracted with his usual roll call.

FRANKIE

```
Is Queens underground?
```

A few people squealed.

FRANKIE

```
Bronx?
```

Not many. Too far away.

FRANKIE

```
What about Harlem?
```

A few more than Queens.

FRANKIE

```
What about Lower East Side?
```

A nice portion of the crowd clapped and hooed.

FRANKIE

```
Okay, okay . . . is Brooklyn in the
house?
```

Boom! You would've thought we were in Brooklyn, judging by the number of people screaming. It's always that way. Sometimes I wonder if everybody really lives in Brooklyn, or if everybody just likes to scream for Brooklyn because it's the cool thing to scream for. I mean, "Is Brooklyn in the house?" has always been a cooler thing to say than any other borough or city in the house. Just is.

Frankie turned around to check on us to see if we were ready. Alexis was finishing up tuning his bass, and everyone else was pretty much set.

A lady shouted from the back of the crowd.

AUSTRALIAN LADY

Melbourne in the house!

Frankie whipped around.

FRANKIE

Who?

The lady jumped up and down in the back, waving her hand.

AUSTRALIAN LADY

Melbourne!

FRANKIE

Melburn? Where is Melburn?

AUSTRALIAN LADY

Australia!

ALEXIS

Australia!

FRANKIE

Oh! You mean Mel-born! You from Mel-born? Mel-born in the house, y'all! Do y'all really ride on kangaroos?

Everybody in the crowd laughed, and it all just went along with Famous Frankie's charm, even though he was dead serious about the whole thing. He shrugged it off, and Keith gave him the signal.

Showtime.

The thing about that station is the crowd was interesting. I mean, every crowd was interesting, but Fourteenth Street was just . . . different. I mean, we had our club kids from the night before, but the new people—the people who were coming underground to take the train because they work in the area or whatever, they were way different.

The neighborhood aboveground was cool but kind of fancy. It's where all the expensive fashion brands were, and the swanky stone streets you always see in pictures of other countries. It's like every other country in the world has streets made of pretty stones, but we just got this asphalt and concrete. Except in this neighborhood.

But not everything was that way—fancy. There were also tons of just regular places like diners and bars, little grocery stores and churches. And a lot of boring buildings that people lived in. So underground, there were really, really cool-looking people, and those people, I assumed, lived somewhere else and were just working at one of those stores.

There were some girls dressed in—I don't know—but it looked uncomfortable, which means it was probably expensive. And some of the guys looked the same, skinny jeans and wing-tip shoes—dudes looked important. These guys and the girls, though killing with the clothes, all looked exhausted. That's how I knew they worked around there.

And then there were other people who just looked super laidback. Sweatpants, easy dresses and sneakers, yoga pants. These folks I figured were the ones who actually could afford to live in this neighborhood. I didn't know how much the rent was, but I knew it had to be pretty high since they had stone streets. And these people didn't look tired at all. Not one bit. An interesting mix.

Tonight, Keith was the lead. Seemed like a good idea since she was so gassed up about playing at Fourteenth Street. Like we were gigging at Madison Square Garden or something.

SG

On you.

KEITH

I got it.

Her smile peeked out from behind both sides of the mouthpiece of her trumpet.

She took a deep breath in and began to blow. The tone started low and slow as Keith dragged the notes, adding a little vibrato on the end as if she was singing a sad bluesy song. Not what we were expecting, but it was gorgeous.

The crowd fell dead silent and just listened as Keith performed. She turned her back on the crowd, the way Miles Davis did, and while she faced me, she winked just to let me know that she knew she was killing.

When the trains would pull in, screeching and grinding, Keith accompanied them with notes that made the sound of metal on metal sound more like music. As people got off, they were instantly hypnotized by this bald-headed, freckle-faced girl, swaying to her own song. Some people tried to walk away, but Keith walked right behind them, begging them with the horn to stay. And when they wouldn't, when a few people really just decided to leave even though she followed them to the stairs (the advantage of not having to sit down or plug nothing in), she flipped it. And began to quack and honk.

I just started laughing as she bounced around quacking and honking, playing short, choppy notes. It was like she was making fun of the "runaways," like she was heckling the people who didn't want to stay for the show.

The audience clapped and laughed at the weird noises, not knowing that it was also Keith's signal to the rest of the band to say "snap out of it, and let's rock," and out of nowhere she ripped into a cool-ass version of "When the Saints Go Marching In." And we were right there to bring the rest of that New Orleans sound to Fourteenth Street.

Before we knew it, Keith and Frankie were leading a dance line, dozens of people following behind them as they marched round and round.

WHEN I GOT HOME that night, Uncle Lucky was sitting on the couch flipping through channels on the television. A drink sat on the table in front of him. It might have been water, or it could've been vodka. Couldn't quite tell. It was late, and usually he was knocked out by then, or at least in his room with the door closed. But on this night, he just sat up, almost like he was waiting for me to come home.

SG

Hey, Unc.

I closed the door behind me. I locked the knob and the dead bolt, and put the chain on.

UNCLE LUCKY

Wassup, kid?

He took a sip from the glass. The face he made let me know that it was definitely vodka.

UNCLE LUCKY

How was the show?

He scooted over so that I could sit down next to him. I kicked my shoes off and leaned back to get comfortable, which I knew was impossible, but I had to try anyway. I was still buzzing from it all.

SG

```
It was crazy. So many people. I mean,
people were clapping when we showed up!
```

Uncle Lucky looked at me sideways.

UNCLE LUCKY

```
Be careful. That asshole is looking
for y'all.
```

SG

```
Dummy?
```

UNCLE LUCKY

```
Yeah. He left here a little while ago.
Let me know the cops were on the case.
```

SG

```
He came here?
```

My uncle looked at me for a second, then cut his eyes back to the television.

UNCLE LUCKY

```
Uh huh.
```

He picked up the remote and channeled up a few times until getting to the cooking channel, which has always been his favorite even though the dude doesn't cook a thing.

UNCLE LUCKY

It took everything in me not to give him round two of what your homeboy gave him.

He glanced back at me.

SG

But what did he say?

UNCLE LUCKY

That they'd find y'all eventually, and when they did, your boy was going down.

Uncle Lucky took another sip of the firewater.

UNCLE LUCKY

You know, your friend can get six months for this mess.

SG

Six months?!

I felt like I could jump out of my skin. I leaned back again, now wishing I could fold myself into the cushion. I mean, maybe Alexis's question was valid. How long could we run? Clearly, this fool was not letting up.

SG

I need you to talk to Mom.

Uncle Lucky sat up again. I had been meaning to talk to him about this, but the past few days had been so busy that I hadn't had a chance to, especially since he's usually asleep pretty early.

SG

I need you to get her to convince him to call off the dogs.

UNCLE LUCKY

What makes you think she's not already trying to get him to chill out?

SG

Because I used to live there. She's different around him. Like he's got some kinda power over her or something. It's sick.

Just saying that made me feel nauseous.

SG

But if you ask her—like *really* ask her—maybe she'll do it.

My uncle put his glass to his lips again, and before taking another sip, asked:

UNCLE LUCKY

Why don't you just ask her yourself?

He dipped his lip into the glass and let the clear liquid slip into his mouth. He strained his neck and swallowed.

SG

Because . . . because I just don't want to talk to her. I got nothing to say to her.

UNCLE LUCKY

`That's still your mother.`

SG

`That's still your baby sister. And to be honest, she's acting a lot more like a baby sister than a mother these days.`

Unc nodded, then shot the rest of his drink. He hissed for a second, then said:

UNCLE LUCKY

`Got a point there, nephew.`

He set the empty glass back on the table.

UNCLE LUCKY

`I'll try my best.`

The thing about the cops is they can find out everything about you. Where you live, where you work, whatever they need to know. So the first thing I did was text Alexis.

yo my moms bf just left here

what he say to u?

wasnt here but he talked to my unc. said the cops will find u

It took Alexis a minute to say anything back, probably because he was flipping out.

what should i do??? should i just give myself up?

I thought about that, but decided against it only because why should my friend, a person who tried to protect my mother, go to jail and the man who hit her walks free to do it again and again?

no. my uncle will fix it. he said he was goin to talk to her. just be careful. we'll talk bout it tmrw.

THE NEXT MORNING I DID my usual super rounds, to fix things in the building for people. I stopped at Ms. Torrie's place to lay mousetraps, Mr. Garcia's place to snake the toilet even though he promised me he would try using the trash can I bought him the week before, and of course, last but not least, I popped into Ms. Dyson's apartment to see if she needed anything from me. Dunks had called me early in the morning, telling me that she had been calling his phone over and over again, but he kept ignoring the call because he just couldn't deal with her while also trying to listen to Carlos Santana.

DUNKS

Dude, "Black Magic Woman" was playing.

I could still hear the guitar blasting through the speaker in the background.

SG

And black magic woman was calling too!

DUNKS

Man, she ain't the kind I'm looking for. Plus, you know it's something stupid like her not knowing that televisions have remote controls, or something wild like that.

SG

Ah, cut her some slack. She's old. And one day we're gonna be old and crazy too.

DUNKS

No, you're gonna be old and crazy. I'm gonna be on Pluto with the rest of my kind, playing astro sounds.

SG

Right.

I knocked on Ms. Dyson's door.

MS. DYSON

Yes? Who is it?

SG

It's Stuyvesant, from downstairs. Just coming to check in on you.

After unlocking everything and telling me to wait right there, as if I was going somewhere, the door swung open.

MS. DYSON

Hey, baby.

She wore purple pants that looked like they had been over-ironed and were stiff as cardboard. They were cut off at the ankle, so I could see her tan stockings that blended right into her tan old lady bad-feet sneakers.

MS. DYSON

Come on in.

She sounded sweet, which was a little weird. I walked in slowly, almost like I was expecting this to be some kind of trap or something.

SG

Any problems or issues, Ms. Dyson?

My eyes darted around the room at all the . . . stuff.

MS. DYSON

Only one.

She walked over to the coffee table that had an ashtray, a cup of what I guessed was cold coffee, a plate with a few crumbs and a banana peel on it, and a newspaper, which would surely be added to the thousands she had stacked along the walls.

She grabbed the paper and held it up.

MS. DYSON

Why didn't you tell me y'all was famous?

SG

Huh?

MS. DYSON

Fay-muss.

I came closer to get a better look at what she was talking about.

And there we were. Well, mainly just Keith and Frankie—Famous Frankie—leading the dance line. Keith's cheeks were swollen with air. Her and Frankie looked like they had choreographed the whole thing—Keith holding the trumpet to her lips, and Frankie, the megaphone to his. In the background, you can see a fuzzy me in full drum mode, except without real drums. Both hands were in the air like I was about to come down with a boom on the bucket in front of me. You could see Dunks too, looking all cracked out, eyes closed, hunched over. But you couldn't really see Alexis. He was way too big for the frame, and so all you could make out was his guitar and his belly.

The headline read: THE SOUND FROM UNDERGROUND, NYC'S SECRET SOUNDTRACK.

MS. DYSON

Here.

Ms. Dyson pushed the paper into my hands.

I stood there and read the article, which basically just said that there was a secret band that plays at night in subway stations and that we were causing "quite a stir."

There were no quotes or names or anything. Just a spotlight. And the writer even went on to say that he purposely didn't interview us or ask us where we were playing next because he thought the fun in the whole thing was in not knowing. Like an adventure underground.

SG

This came today?

I was feeling super excited and also really nervous at the same time. I mean, it was awesome to be recognized as some kind of . . . thing. Like a movement. That was cool, especially since the crowds were getting bigger and bigger and so was the money. I mean, from the first Union Square show to now, we were at about two thousand dollars, putting us a few thousand away from having enough to go into a big studio and record a real album.

But on the flip side, this was the newspaper. Everybody in New York read the newspaper. Even Dummy.

Even cops. And that's what I was most worried about.

MS. DYSON

So when are you and Duncan doing your next show?

Ms. Dyson gestured for her newspaper. I gave it back, and she folded it in half and slapped it on her leg.

MS. DYSON

Maybe I'll come out there and see y'all.

I smiled and played along, still feeling all jittery inside.

SG

You gonna come see us, Ms. Dyson?

MS. DYSON

Maybe. Just depends if the train wants to run for me.

SG

The train runs for everybody.

MS. DYSON

Everybody but me.

She shook her head. Instead of even entertaining that, I just ignored her and moved on with the conversation.

SG

Well, I don't know where we'll be anyway, and we wouldn't want you wandering around looking for us at night, y'know?

MS. DYSON

Yeah, a lot of scary stuff happens out there these days.

She walked into the kitchen. I heard her open a drawer and begin digging around. If I'd had to guess what was in that drawer, I would say it was the same kinds of things that were in the drawer in my mom's kitchen—even in my uncle's kitchen. Staplers, scissors, twist ties, tape, old photos of old friends, corkscrews. Things like that.

MS. DYSON

You know it's kids out there with all kinds of things stuck in their faces. It's frightening.

Her deep, scratchy voice was suddenly adorable.

I wanted to laugh. I mean, I should've laughed because it was funny. But I couldn't because I was getting anxious, number 1, because I was just standing in Ms. Dyson's weird apartment, and number 2, because I really wanted to go tell everybody we were in the newspaper.

But Ms. Dyson kept yapping. Questions about the band, how long we've been playing, if we're going to make an album, do we think we'll be featured in *Ebony* or *Jet*, yadda yadda yadda. Back and forth from the kitchen to the living room, searching for something, until finally she found it buried in the bottom of her soft pink purse (or as she called it, her "pockybook"), which was big enough to cover damn near an entire couch cushion. A marker! I was trying to leave, and she asked me to autograph her newspaper. She pointed the marker at me like it was a magic wand and she was casting a spell.

SG

Seriously?

MS. DYSON

Yeah, child. You famous, aintcha?

Her eyes were old, but still sweet. They looked like they had seen a lot through the years. Some good. Some not so good. It was the not so good that made me give in.

SG

Okay, but then I gotta run and check on the other tenants.

She smiled and held the paper out, our picture big as day, right there. I took the marker, and for the first time, I scribbled what I thought was the coolest way to write Stuyvesant Grey.

Down the steps. Down the steps. Down all the freakin' steps! When I got to Dunks's door, I banged. I knew he wouldn't hear me because of his music blasting as usual, but I banged and banged and banged until he finally opened the door.

He stood there, shirtless, holding a huge bowl of cereal that he was eating with an equally big spoon.

DUNKS

```
What's wrong?
```

He noticed me all out of breath, clearly freaking out.

SG

```
Come . . . Come with me.
```

I was panting, trying to catch my wind. Then I tore off down the steps, bursting out of the building as if I was being chased by something.

Dunks came out a few seconds after me, still shirtless. It was like you could see all the muscles and organs in his body, moving and working with every step.

DUNKS

```
What's wrong, dude? Did Ms. Dyson do
something to you?
```

SG

```
No, man.
```

I walked down the block. Dunks followed behind asking where we were going, and once we got to a newsstand, I grabbed a paper, opened it up, and showed Dunks why I was freaking.

SG

```
Look.
```

I dug in my pocket for a few bucks. I slapped the crumpled dollars on the counter.

Dunks stared at the paper, his lips moving as he read the headline, his eyes jumping as he studied the photo.

DUNKS

Oh shit. Is that . . . Is that us?

SG

Uh huh.

DUNKS

Yo, Stuy, that's us! That's really us!

Dunks started jumping around, laughing and bumping me like we had just scored a touchdown. The guy behind the stand opened the newspaper and checked it out for himself. We looked around at other people walking with their coffee and their cigarettes, and that paper tucked under their arms, knowing that they had either already seen us, or were going to see us once they got in their cabs or took a seat on the train.

DUNKS

Oh man.

He shoved a few fingers into the pockets of his skintight jeans.

DUNKS

Look at Frankie. He really is famous now!

When he yanked his fingers out, dollar bills fell from his pockets like dried-up leaves. I bent down to help him pick them up. He tucked the paper he was holding—my paper—under his arm and counted out the ones.

DUNKS

. . . Six, seven, eight.

He smoothed the stack of bills out with his thumb and put them down on the newsstand counter.

DUNKS

```
Four more, please.
```

His face was glowing with excitement.

When we got back to his place, we started texting everybody, starting with the rest of the band.

I literally copied and pasted WE IN THE PAPER! to Keith, Alexis, Frankie, even Dylan, then to everyone else in my phone, just going down the list from old band friends from high school, my old band teacher Mr. Rochester, my uncle Lucky. But I had to stop when I got to my mom.

I wanted to tell her so bad. I knew despite everything going on, she'd still be happy for me. And also it would be kind of a way for me to say "I told you so," and considering how I had been feeling lately, there was nothing I wanted to say more than that. Y'know, to prove a point. Well, really just to remind her that the music still works. It still moves people. The paper called us "New York City's house band." We were the sound of the city.

But I couldn't do it. I couldn't text her. Plus, I knew she'd see the paper anyways.

It wasn't long before the replies started pouring in.

My uncle hit me right away.

UNCLE LUCKY

looking at it right now!

proud of you nephew!

KEITH

look at me, killin' em! :)

Alexis just texted that he'd call me in a minute, which I thought was weird because he normally would be heading to the printshop for work.

While I was scrolling through all the replies, including one from my band teacher telling me how proud he was of me that I stuck with the music (I needed that), Dunks had already cut out the clip and nailed it to his wall. He actually nailed it. With a hammer. I don't know why he couldn't just use a tack or a piece of tape. Instead he used a big nail and drove it straight through the *O* in UNDERGROUND. Then he sat on the dingy couch, crossed his legs, and stared at it.

SG

```
Crazy, right?
```

I sat next to him to stare for a while myself. I have to admit, it was like staring at a freeze-frame in a movie, starring us.

DUNKS

```
Dude. I can't even believe it.
```

He grabbed his guitar and laid it on his lap, strings down. He bent over and swept the floor with his hand until he found another nail.

SG

```
What you doin?
```

Dunks ignored me and started scraping the nail across the back of the neck of his pink guitar. He dug it into the wood and yanked it back and forth, each carve making me cringe. I mean, this was his baby—his Pepto Bismol girlfriend.

Every two minutes he would lift his head and look at the newspaper clip, and mumble:

DUNKS

```
It's time.
```

Such a weirdo.

But what he was doing, which I didn't realize until he was finished, was carving SOUNDTRACK into the wood. It had been three months, pretty much a whole summer, and this was like Dunks giving his guitar a tattoo, a stamp that we were not just *a* band, but a *real* band.

CHAPTER 12

STUY'S MOM

do not play 14th street tonight

THIS WAS A TEXT MESSAGE THAT CAME THROUGH FROM my mother about an hour after we saw the newspaper. At first, I thought it was a threat.

But then I realized that it was actually a warning.

I texted back OK. I wanted to ask her if she'd seen it, even though I knew she had, which is why she was sending me the warning in the first place. But still, I wanted to know what she thought about it. If she was proud. But I didn't ask her any of this. I just texted her again, this time just Thanks.

Alexis finally called me. He explained that he saw the paper, and how this was good for us, but bad for him.

SG

I know. That was the first thing I thought about. Everybody knows we play down there now. Everybody.

ALEXIS

Exactly.

His phone voice made him sound a lot smaller.

ALEXIS

```
So I’m screwed.
```

Dunks and I were sitting at the Spanish spot. I wasn’t eating, but Dunks was stuffing his face with plantains.

SG

```
You at work?
```

ALEXIS

```
Work? Hell no. I called out, because I’m
sure the cops will be checking for me
there today. My ass ain’t leaving the
house, knowhatimsayin’?
```

SG

```
But we need to meet.
```

ALEXIS

```
Then we meeting over here.
```

The ride to Brooklyn is a quick one from the Lower East Side, but I hadn’t made the trip since I had left my mom’s house a few months before. And judging by how Dunks was looking around when we got off the train, I wasn’t sure if he had ever been across the bridge a day in his life.

SG

```
This is Brooklyn, man.
```

DUNKS

`I know!`

He was trying to act like he was comfortable. Like it was no big deal.

DUNKS

`Home of Biggie.`

SG

`What? What you know about Biggie?`

I was shocked that he mentioned the Brooklyn emcee. Dunks stopped walking.

DUNKS

It was all a dream. I used to read *Word Up* magazine.

He was rapping in a weird low voice and waving his arms around awkwardly.

SG

`Okay, okay, okay, you know Biggie.`

I tried to get him to shut up. People were looking at him—this tall lanky hipster kid—like he was from another planet. Or worse, another neighborhood.

We walked from block to block, across Atlantic Avenue, until we finally reached our destination. The Albany projects.

There's a rule about the projects: Don't go there unless you live there, and if you don't live there, you better know somebody who does and have them come escort you in. I used to think it had something to do with just picking on people on the outside trying to get in, but now I thought it just had to do with protecting the people on the inside. Like the projects was a big clubhouse, and if you didn't have a club card or know a password, you weren't allowed in.

The thing about this clubhouse was that it seemed scary as hell. And if I was a little shook, Dunks was damn near about to pass out.

As we walked up to the door, guys sat outside on benches, passing blunts back and forth, a stereo at their feet blasting a song I had never heard. It sounded like it had been recorded in a closet.

They looked at us for a second and nodded. I nodded back and kept it moving as calm as possible. As long as they didn't ask us anything, we were fine. And they didn't ask us anything. So no big deal.

Once we got to the door, Dunks let out a huge sigh. I think he had been holding his breath the whole time.

SG

`You aight?`

I hit the up button on the elevator.

DUNKS

`Uh huh.`

He stood right up on the elevator doors like a weirdo. When they finally opened, a dude was standing right there, and Dunks almost collided into him. Probably would've kissed the dude right in the mouth. What did Dunks do?

DUNKS

`AAAAAHHHHH!`

RANDOM TENANT

What the hell?

The guy slid past him, annoyed and confused.

SG

Sorry, man.

I pushed Dunks into the elevator and told him to get himself together.

SG

Yo, man, you might not believe this, but people who live here are people just like you. So chill out.

I pushed the button for the twelfth floor. Once off the elevator, we walked down the hall until we got to 12G. We knocked on the door. No answer. We knocked again, this time harder. Still, no answer.

A dude and a girl stood at the end of the hallway talking. He kept pulling her closer to him, and she kept pushing away. Back and forth. Then they looked at us and we looked away, but not in time. They caught us, and the guy yelled out something, but neither me or Dunks knew what he said. Dunks opened his mouth like he was about to ask the guy to repeat himself.

SG

Don't. Not a word. Just knock on the door again, and I'm gonna text him.

I yanked my phone from my pocket. A few seconds after pushing SEND, we heard all the unlocking.

Alexis's apartment was cool, but you would've never known that there were any parents who lived here. There were posters of basses and bass players all over the walls. In the corner were stacked Marshall amplifiers and a pile of cords like a snake pit. There was a big couch in the middle of the living room, which was where Dunks and I sat.

ALEXIS

Man, I don't open the door for no knocks. Gotta text me so I can make sure you ain't the cops.

Alexis was sitting on the arm of the couch. He was drinking water out of a gallon jug.

SG

What about your folks? Do they know about what's going on?

ALEXIS

Naw, man. They don't need to know.

SG

So what happens if they're here and the cops come knocking? What's gonna keep them from opening the door?

Alexis turned the jug up and guzzled for a few seconds. Then he wiped his mouth and belched.

ALEXIS

They can't hear it.

SG

```
Oh snap, that's right.
```

I totally forgot his parents were deaf.

ALEXIS

```
But they already know about the
newspaper clip. They saw it this morning
with the rest of the city. My dad sent
me this video message.
```

Alexis fiddled with his phone for a second, then handed it to me. On the screen was a round-faced brown-skinned man, with white stubble covering his chin and cheeks, cheesing. He held the paper up and pointed to Alexis's stomach. Then he made a few signs with his hands, then busted out laughing. Then he gave a thumbs up, and the message ended.

DUNKS

```
What did he say?
```

Alexis grinned.

ALEXIS

```
He said, "I see Keith's big head, so I
assume this is your belly."
```

Alexis set the gallon jug on the table.

ALEXIS

```
But that smile on his face says the
most.
```

DUNKS

Yeah, man, Pops looks pretty hype.

Dunks and I both looked at the freeze-frame of Alexis's father's face. Then we handed the phone back to Alexis.

ALEXIS

Man, that's nothing. Look at this.

Alexis swiped over his phone a few times and then handed it back to us.

ALEXIS

That's my mom.

It was a photo of his mother, a really, really pretty woman kissing the newspaper.

ALEXIS

And that's why I can't tell them about everything that's going on.

SG

I hear you. My uncle said he would try to get my mother to get her crazy boyfriend to relax, but he hasn't yet. As a matter fact, she texted me this morning saying not to play at Fourteenth today.

ALEXIS

Of course not! Man, I'm going nowhere near that place.

DUNKS

So what are we gonna do?

Dunks was up and walking over to the corner where the amps were.

DUNKS

I mean, this is like our dream come true and our worst nightmare at the same time.

ALEXIS

My worst nightmare.

Alexis sat back on the arm of the couch and let himself slip down into the cushions.

SG

Our worst nightmare.

I was making sure Alexis understood we were all in this together.

SG

I've been thinking about what we're gonna do. I'm just waiting until Keith and Frankie get here.

For the next hour or so, me and Dunks killed time by asking Alexis a million questions about his parents being deaf. I mean, I never knew any deaf people, so it was all pretty fascinating. After we asked him how they knew the phone was ringing, he said:

ALEXIS

Watch this.

He took his cell phone and dialed his house, and when the house phone started ringing, the lights started flashing.

ALEXIS

Same thing happens when their alarm goes off in the morning.

SG

Straight-up amazing.

He also showed us how to sign S-O-U-N-D-T-R-A-C-K, which was way harder than I thought it was going to be. Of course, for Alexis, it was nothing as he flipped his fingers every which way like he was throwing up gang signs.

SG

Dude, that's incredible.

DUNKS

Seriously.

ALEXIS

Thanks. I guess it all ended up helping with my instrument. Y'know, being able to talk with my hands.

SG

Right.

ALEXIS

Matter fact, let me show you guys how it works in here. Like, how I play for my folks.

Alexis got up and plugged in his bass, then flung it over his shoulder and around his neck. He hiked it up and rested it on his belly as usual, then turned one of the amplifiers on.

ALEXIS

Okay, now y'all come over here and lean against the wall.

He put his hand along the wall that led down a hallway to which I figured were the bedrooms. I could see the grease stain from his parents' heads on the wall, one lower than the other. Then he played "Mary Had a Little Lamb." I could feel every note tingling down my back, and the rumble from the bass made me feel like my stomach was vibrating on the inside. I looked over at Dunks, and he had his hands over his ears, I guess trying to see what it would be like if he couldn't hear.

It wasn't until Alexis stopped playing that we heard his phone vibrating on the table.

DUNKS

Yo, that was amazing.

Dunks took his hands from the side of his head.

SG

Yeah, man. That's pretty dope.

I watched Alexis check his phone. Then he unplugged the bass and walked over to the front door. Unlocked it all and cracked it. A few seconds later, Keith and Frankie walked in. Keith howled, holding the paper up.

KEITH

Yoooooo. This is bananas!

SG

I know, right? Your ug-mug is all over the newspaper!

I put Frankie in a headlock. Frankie laughed and pushed me away.

FRANKIE

Yo, I'm gonna have to sign mad autographs now.

KEITH

Yeah, as soon as I'm done signing mine.

DUNKS

Please, once they see this next solo I got for 'em, there won't even be such a thing as autographs. Just astro-graphs.

Dunks held his fingers up to his head like a freak.

KEITH

Shut up!

SG

Please!

ALEXIS

Everybody shut up!

We kept laughing, until we realized that Alexis wasn't laughing at all. He was serious. He leaned his bass against the wall and sat on the floor next to it. He stared at the floor.

SG

Yo, Alexis is right. What we have to do is figure out what we're gonna do now.

I looked around at everyone, their eyes all on me.

SG

We *have* to keep playing. I mean, we just have to.

KEITH

We have to.

SG

But we also have to look out for our boy.

KEITH

Exactly.

Frankie went over and sat next to Alexis, who at this point looked like he was on the verge of crying. Frankie put his thirteen-year-old arm around the big guy's neck, like a toddler hugging a tree trunk.

SG

I have an idea. Tonight we don't play. We can't. It's just too hot now. Cops are probably gonna be all over the place.

DUNKS

So what's your plan?

SG

I say we hit Dylan, and tell her to let people know that we'll be playing tomorrow, but that she has to make sure she whispers it in people's ears. It has to stay a secret because like the newspaper said, that's kind of part of the whole thing.

My bandmates all looked at me. Dunks looked like he was cool with it, but Keith looked unsure.

KEITH

But where are we telling Dylan to tell people we're playing? We can't just show up the next day at Fourteenth like everything is all good.

She slid down the wall, plopping onto the floor too.

SG

I know we can't. That's why we tell her we're going far away. Uptown. Harlem, 125th Street.

They all sat in silence, and I just waited for it all to sink in. I knew this was a good idea. I knew it would work. All we needed was for Dylan to do what she had already been doing so well for us and then hope that people would travel uptown to see us. And because of the newspaper hype, we had a good shot. Either way, we could keep Alexis straight for at least another week, which I hoped would be enough time for my uncle to work his magic on my mom. All I needed was for the team to believe, and all that was going to take was for one of them to speak up and agree.

And someone did. The perfect person. Alexis.

ALEXIS

I'm down. Let's do it.

Alexis reached up, calling for me to come grab his hand. I clasped it tight and pulled as hard as I could to help him get to his feet.

KEITH

If Alexis is in, I'm in.

I looked at Frankie, who looked at Keith. I knew if she was in, he was too.

SG

Dunks?

DUNKS

I'm good with it.

ALEXIS

Text Dylan. Let her know that tomorrow, Soundtrack is taking over Harlem.

* * *

THAT NIGHT, I SAT on the couch in my uncle's house, in my underwear, eating ramen noodles, watching YouTube clips of Savion. I had seen most of them already. Had studied them inside and out. But there was one clip that I loved to watch, that always came up whenever I typed in his name, even though he doesn't actually dance in it.

It's from this movie that came out back in the eighties called *Tap*, and the clip that always comes up is from this part in the movie where all these old tap dancers are getting busy—I think they're challenging Gregory Hines—and Savion, who was a little boy at the time, was just watching. I always thought it was so dope to see those old heads sliding across the floor, stomping and clicking their feet, smooth as ever.

I watched that clip a few times. First with my eyes closed, listening to the rhythms that their feet were making. Then, with my eyes open so I could see what it's like to be black and old and cool as hell. Which got me checking for other old clips. I typed in MOTOWN, and checked a bunch of old clips of bands like the Temptations and the Supremes. Stevie Wonder. Jackson 5. Marvin Gaye. On and on, listening to the drums, looking at the people, their moves, their swagger.

I sat and watched, typing in as many old school groups as I could think of until I was all out.

That's when I typed a name in the search bar that I had never typed before. A band I had strangely never even thought about searching for: the Bed-Stuy Magic Dusters.

There was one clip. Only one. Every other clip that came up had something to do with vacuum cleaners, or something stupid like that. But, again, there was one: BED-STUY MAGIC DUSTERS LIVE AT CBGB, 1991. The song was called "Rotten Apple." I pushed play.

VINCE

```
We are the Bed-Stuy Magic Dusters! Yeah,
yeah. CBGB, let me hear you if you came
here to get dusted. Uh huh, I said, let me
hear you if y'all came here to get dusted!
```

Whoever was filming had a tight shot on the high-pitched guy on the mic. His name was Vince. My mother told me all about him a long time ago. She always said he was one of the best punk singers she had ever heard. He was short and stocky, and on the video clip he already had his shirt off and wore tight little cutoff jean shorts. His face looked lumpy, like it was all bone and no fat. Sunken in like a skeleton. Perfect for a punk band. Vince's mouth was pressed right up on the mic as he charged up the crowd.

VINCE

```
Y'all ready to get dusted?
```

The crowd screamed. From there, the camera panned back, and my eyes shot straight to the back to see the drummer. My mother. I couldn't believe it. She looked just like she looked now, but just younger. Happier. Her thick hair was all over her head as she ripped into the song, hard and fast, her arms swinging as the band threw down:

VINCE

```
New York City only pities the pretty
But on the gritty they close the door
And it ain't just the skin, we bruised within
This apple is rotten . . .
```

My mother rolled out on the drums before the whole crowd screamed:

CROWD

. . . DOWN TO THE CORE!

It wasn't until after the first verse that I noticed the bass player. My father. A man I had seen in whatever pictures my mom had, which weren't many. But now I was sitting there in front of my computer looking at this guy. This jerk. This musician. Both of my parents onstage rocking out. It was like looking at myself, what I'm made of.

I played the clip over and over again, loving the song, watching my mother, watching my father, watching my father nod and wink at my mother, the whole thing.

It's hard to really explain what it felt like. There was part of me upset that my mom let go of this part of her—the music. But I'm sure it must've been tough for her after everything that happened with the way they split up. And having me.

There was another part of me, though, that felt kind of proud about what I was seeing. I mean, the Dusters were no joke!

The wildest part of it all was what it said in the caption under the clip: *A piece of footage from my dad's (the bass player's) old band, the Bed-Stuy Magic Dusters. RIP Daddy, aka Bottom.*

What. The. Hell. I stared at the screen, those words. Could it be? Really?

You know how you start feeling crazy, second-guessing yourself about things you know for sure aren't true. I started doing that whole thing. Like: *Did my mother show me this footage a while back and I posted it on YouTube and wrote that caption, and just forgot?* Followed by: *Of course not, fool! You've never even seen this a day in your life!* Plus I didn't even know Bottom was dead. And even though I honestly had no intention of ever finding him, it still stung a little to know that the possibility was off the table forever.

My brain was melting, and for about five minutes I sat there on the couch thinking about emailing this person to find out who they were, where they were, something. I mean, I had never had any brothers and sisters. I figured it would be cool to know that someone out there was connected to me like that. But then I thought about my crew, my band. I thought about Alexis the protector, Keith the tough sister, Dunks the awkward child, and Famous Frankie the baby of the bunch, and realized that I was okay. I was connected. I had family already.

So I closed the laptop and went to sleep.

CHAPTER 13

OKAY, SO ABOUT WHAT I SAID ABOUT CLOSING THE LAPTOP and going to sleep. That didn't actually happen. I mean, I did close the laptop, but I didn't go to sleep. Because I opened the laptop again. Just to watch the video one more time, before clicking on the name of the person who posted it.

The screen name was magicdustisamust, which I thought was kinda corny. But whatever. The option for SEND MESSAGE came up. I clicked on it. But what was I going to say? What was there to say? *Hey, whoever you are out there. We got the same pops.* No. Definitely not that. *If Bottom was your father, then I'm your brother.* Meh. Maybe. *Hey . . . who the hell are you and where the hell have you been?* This one made me laugh.

I started typing.

Dear magicdustisamust,

My name is Stuyvesant Grey. My mother's name is Gloria Grey. She was the drummer for the Bed-Stuy Magic Dusters.

I thought about stopping there, thinking maybe whoever this person was, they would put two and two together. But Bottom might have never even mentioned that he was dating my mom back then. So I continued:

> When I searched and found this video, I couldn't believe my eyes. I had heard this music a few times growing up. My mother would play it for me as she was teaching me to play the drums. So to actually see her doing her thing—

I deleted *doing her thing.* Didn't want to sound too comfortable with my stranger-sibling.

> So to actually see her performing really made my day. The other thing about seeing this footage is that it gave me a chance to see both of my parents together. See, and this is going to sound crazy, but my father played for the Magic Dusters too. He played bass. His name was Bottom.
>
> So . . . I think we might be siblings. I'm not expecting you to really reply. I've seen enough TV shows to know that this kind of thing can be a bit much. But when I saw your caption, I at least had to say something.
>
> Sincerely, Stuy Grey

I read it over a few times. I have to say, I sounded pretty awesome. Confident, but not cocky. SEND.

I lay back on the couch, the laptop screen shining on me. I couldn't sleep. It felt like my body had become its own drum set, my heart banging like a bass drum and my brain crashing like cymbals. What would they think? Maybe they would think it was a joke or a prank. Some internet weirdo doing some late-night spamming.

I tried to block it all out, to pretend like I didn't care because most likely no one would respond. I knew if it were me receiving a message like that, I would think it was some kind of joke. Like, *Hey, you got a long-lost brother. Surprise!* Yeah, right.

Maybe six minutes went by. Maybe. Might've been less, when I rolled over and glanced at the screen.

Inbox (1) From: magicdustisamust

Oh. My. God. I sprang up and moved to the edge of the couch. My body—the drum set—was in the middle of the meanest solo of its life. I couldn't believe that whoever was on the other end of that video was now on the other end of this email. They had written me back! I took a deep breath and clicked.

Dear Stuyvesant,

Whoa. So, I'm definitely surprised, but honestly, I believe you. My dad did tell me that he had dated your mom, but he never said he had a kid with her. But I Googled you a minute ago, and a picture of you from high school popped up. I think it was your senior year, school band photo. You look just like him. You look just like me, except a little older, and you're a boy. I don't really know what else to write. I'm just shocked.

Crazy, Ashley

A girl. My little sister. Ashley. I sat there for a second and just smiled at the words on the screen. Then I wrote back.

Ashley,

There's so much I want to say. So many questions. So I'm just going to start, and you answer what you want.

1) What was our father like?

2) How old are you? I'm eighteen.

3) I was told Bottom moved to the West Coast. Are you in Cali?

4) This is the most important question. Do you like music?

Stuy

A few minutes slowly ticked by and my curiosity was driving me nuts, so I got up and went to the kitchen for a glass of water. I pounded it back, water dripping down my chin and chest. I put the glass in the sink, panted, belched. I wasn't even really thirsty. Guzzling water was just the only thing I could think of to take my mind off the computer.

I sat back on the couch. She had replied, thank God.

Stuy,

Our dad was a trip. But he was okay. I'll tell you this, the man loved his music, and put it first most of the time, leaving me and my mother to do a lot of stuff on our own. But when he was around, he was awesome. Everything was a joke to him, like he never really grew up. I always liked that about him. He was an easy guy to love, but a hard guy to get to know, if that makes sense. Like I said, the music was everything to him. It was the one thing he took seriously.

You're eighteen? I'm sixteen. Bottom moved pretty quick, I guess.

Cali? We never lived in California. We never lived on the West Coast, period. I've never even been there. Maybe some of the other band members did. I'm not sure. But I've lived in the Bronx my whole life.

And yes, I love music. I didn't really have a choice. Of course, I started out on the bass, so that's my main instrument. But about a year ago, Dad had me working with him in the studio. Oh, I guess I should tell you about that.

A few years back, Dad landed a gig playing for some big movie score. It was a horror flick, so the bass was almost like the lead instrument. He got a pretty big lump from that, and he took it and built a studio in the basement of our house. My mother wasn't really happy about it, but he told her it was a way for me to learn the behind-the-scenes stuff in music so that I wouldn't have to live the life he lived, pinching pennies and all that.

So he built a state-of-the-art studio and taught me how to run it. Right now, I just have my friends come over and we record stupid stuff, but when I'm done with school, I'm really going to try to put Magic Dust Studios on the map.

What about you? Where do you live? Still play music? In a band?

Ash

The Bronx. My father had lived in the Bronx all this time. That part stung worse than hearing that he was dead. I mean, to think that this man, the other half of me, lived a train ride away was pretty messed up. I thought he was on the other side of the country, which for me as a kid might as well have been the other side of the world. But he was literally neighborhoods away. The upside was that this new person, my sister, was close.

Ashley,

I can't believe you guys have been in the Bronx all this time. I'm from Brooklyn. Been there my whole life, until recently when I moved in with my uncle on the Lower East Side. I can't help but wish that I had known you sooner. That I had known him. I've never heard his voice, or anything. He seems like he was an okay guy, and it would've been dope to at least talk music with him.

I wanted to tell her how Bottom left my mother when she was pregnant with me, but it didn't seem necessary. Why mess up the way she feels about her dad? That wouldn't be so cool. It was like my big-brother instincts were already kicking in.

Of course I play. It's in my genes. Lol. And I'm in a band. We call ourselves Soundtrack. It's basically like a crazy jam band. We've only been playing together for a little while, but we're picking up pretty fast.

It's cool that Bottom taught you all the studio stuff, and that he sorta left that to you. That's pretty sweet—a girl who runs a state-of-the-art studio. It's pretty interesting to hear you say that he wanted you to have something to fall back on. My mother pulled the same crap on me. But at least your fallback is something dope and still dealing with music.

Hey, I know this might be crazy to ask, but I'm going to ask anyway. My band is playing tomorrow in Harlem. That's closer to you than where we normally play. You wanna come check us out? If you don't, I understand. It's all pretty crazy. But it would be cool.

Stuy

Stuy,

Yeah, I'll come check you guys! Where in Harlem?

Ash

Ash,

We do this thing where we play in subway stations. Underground. It's like a secret show type of thing, where people show up to see us based on word of mouth. I know it sounds weird, but that's how it works. There are people who follow us everywhere, showing up at every show based on rumors of where we're playing. It's pretty wild. So tomorrow, we're at the 125th Street station on the A line. Around 8-ish.

Stuy

Wait. You play with that secret pop-up band? The one in the newspaper?

My mother brought it to me and was like, "Your father would've loved this." I'm looking at it right now. That's you, fuzzy in the back? I can't believe this! I'll totally be there.

This is so funny. And so unreal. I can't wait to meet you tomorrow.

Love, Ash

CHAPTER 14

I WOKE UP LATE THE NEXT DAY. SAT UP, READ OVER THE conversation I had had with Ashley just to make sure I wasn't dreaming. It was weird to know that her mother brought her the newspaper clipping and said that her father—*our* father—would've loved it. That did something to me. Something different. It kinda pumped me up, like me and Ashley's conversation was the greatest pep talk of all time.

I got up, took a shower, and headed across the hall to Dunks's place. It was Harlem Day, and we had all decided to meet up early.

SG

```
Hey, man.
```

We did our secret shake. Dunks had his usual look of exhaustion, which all of us had just gotten used to. I really don't think he ever slept. At least not much. I think, for him, playing was way more important than sleeping.

He had his guitar on the floor and was in the process of restringing it. He sat back down on the floor and continued knocking the wiry strings into the body of the guitar. I took a seat on the couch and looked at that newspaper clipping of us nailed to the wall.

I pulled the sticks from my back pocket and twirled one in the air. Then I drummed on my legs the best I could what I heard my mother doing in that video of the Magic Dusters.

SG

Yo, you wanna see something sweet?

Dunks was quiet. He got like that whenever he was focused. He called it tapping into his alien self. Like some kind of meditation.

DUNKS

What?

I went over to Dunks's computer and pulled up the clip.

SG

Check this out.

The grainy video came on, and we watched as my mother and father's band rocked the hell out of CBGB. Dunks bobbed his head, staring at the screen like he was looking at live footage from the moon.

DUNKS

What is this?

SG

Hold on.

Then I screamed along with everyone else:

SG

DOWN TO THE CORE!

Then to Dunks:

SG

That's my folks, man! My mom on the drums. And my pops on the bass!

Dunks's mouth hung open as we replayed the video. It was so good. So damn good.

DUNKS

Dude, this is amazing.

SG

I know. And the wild part about it all is that the person who posted it is my little sister!

DUNKS

I didn't know you had a little sister.

SG

I didn't know either! Found out by this video.

I pointed to her screen name, magicdustisamust.

SG

We talked over email all night. And she said she's coming to the show tonight!

DUNKS

That's crazy.

Dunks dropped back to the floor to finish stringing his ax. A poster of Jimi Hendrix was taped to the ceiling, looking down on him.

DUNKS

Then you better not suck tonight.

SG

Man, I never suck, sucker.

I hit play one more time.

VINCE

We are the Bed-Stuy Magic Dusters! Yeah, yeah. CBGB, let me hear you.

A few hours later, everyone else showed up. Keith came in talking trash about how Alexis was walking down the street acting crazy.

KEITH

Yo, this dude was literally walking like he was trying to hide from someone. Like, I would turn around and he'd be standing behind a street meat cart or something.

She set her trumpet case on the floor, walked over to the newspaper clip of us, kissed her fingers, and then pressed them up against the photo of herself.

Alexis leaned his bass case against the wall.

ALEXIS

Whatever. Are there or are there not people out there looking for me?

KEITH

Yes. People looking for you, know what I'm sayin', but there's no point in acting silly about it. I mean, you can at least try to be normal instead of creeping around. We walking down Rivington, and this dude is scaring the white people, tiptoeing, sneaking around and stuff.

The thought of Alexis trying to sneak anywhere was just ridiculous. A guy his size trying to hide is like trying to throw a baby blanket over a building. Just makes no sense.

Frankie plopped down on the couch.

SG

You aight, Frankie?

I noticed that he hadn't really said much. He gave the secret shake when he came in, but that was about it.

FRANKIE

Not feeling too well. Headache.

SG

Hey, Dunks, you got meds in here?

KEITH

```
He’s already had some. I gave him some
aspirin. Should kick in in a minute.
```

She glanced at Alexis, who was sitting on the floor drawing DEFF on random takeout menus Dunks had lying around.

KEITH

```
And if it doesn’t, we’ll send ninja boy
over here to get some more.
```

Alexis balled up one of the menus and beamed it at Keith, just missing her. Then he looked over at me.

ALEXIS

```
Oh, that’s funny, Stuy?
```

SG

```
No, not funny at all.
```

After I showed them the video of my mom’s band about forty times, and we laughed and joked a little more, we eventually got around to practicing and jamming a little. I bammed out that punk rhythm my mom played, hard and fast, while Alexis joined in, strumming his bass as fast he could to keep up with me.

Dunks ran around, slamming into walls as he played power chords, freestyling the silliest lyrics of all time.

DUNKS

```
There’s always something wrong
She says there’s nothing right
```

She always calls my phone all day
and all damn night
Ms. Dyson . . . YOU'RE KILLING ME!

SG, DUNKS, ALEXIS

YOU'RE KILLING ME, MS. DYSON,
YOU'RE KILLING ME!
YOU'RE KILLING ME, MS. DYSON,
YOU'RE KILLING ME!
YOU'RE KILLING ME, MS. DYSON,
YOU'RE KILLING ME!

Keith just sat on the couch, looking at us fools, while Frankie lay in her lap. She rubbed his back like my mother used to do to me whenever I was sick. And just like I used to be, Frankie was knocked out, which was crazy because we were playing pretty loud and for at least an hour.

Six-thirty. Time to get ready to head out. Usually Frankie would've reminded us and got us all focused, but he was still asleep and we decided to leave him alone until it was time to go. Alexis packed his bass back in its black case, and Dunks packed all his gear. The cords. The car battery for the amps. The megaphone.

When it was time to go, we tried waking Frankie up, but he was out cold. So Alexis decided to kill two birds with one stone. He lifted Frankie up and threw him over his shoulder, making sure his face was hidden. But nobody knew what Alexis looked like anyway. It's not like his face was in the newspaper. If anything, he might get stopped by the cops for trying to kidnap the kid they saw in the article!

We headed out, Frankie slung over Alexis's shoulder, but thankfully, by the time we got to the train, Frankie was up.

ALEXIS

```
I can still keep you up here if you
want.
```

Alexis put Frankie down. Keith cut her eyes at Alexis.

FRANKIE

```
Naw, I'm okay. I don't need any of my
fans seeing me that way.
```

He smiled and straightened out his shirt.

The ride to Harlem was a strange one only because it was packed with other subway performers. It was Friday, and for subway performers, they knew on Fridays everybody got paid, which meant they could get paid too.

The breakdancers. These guys were literally doing backflips on a moving train. We'd all seen it a bunch of times, but when you got a kid kicking his legs so close to all of your instruments, you couldn't help but freak out a little. It was one of those situations where we felt like anything could happen to blow this gig for us. The biggest gig yet.

Then there were the drummers, the conga players. They were rocking, and I joined in with my sticks rocking on the poles, which I think might have gotten those dudes a lot more money than they would've made without me.

Then there were the candy boys, selling refreshments for the train show. Snickers. Fruit snacks. And of course, the little boy who wore black pants, a dirty white V-neck T-shirt, white socks, and penny loafers and did his best impression of Michael Jackson, which happened to be the worst impression of Michael Jackson anyone had ever seen. All the kid really wanted to show was that he had mastered the Moonwalk. That was the best part. Everything else . . . not Michael Jackson. Oh, and right before we got off, there was the homeless comedian. I'd seen him a few times, and he was actually pretty dope.

COMEDIAN

```
Yeah, yeah, I hope y'all have enjoyed
your stay in my home. I don't know who
let y'all in, but make sure you cut the
lights out when you leave.
```

Finally we were there, 125th Street. Harlem. We struggled to get all our crap off the train, and a bunch of people filed out after us. 125th is one of those high-traffic stations mainly because it's smack dab in the middle of a historic neighborhood.

As we moved toward the middle of the station, we noticed that a lot of people that got off the train with us were walking right behind us, and when we found a place to set up, they stopped walking and just stood around.

I looked around.

SG

```
You think?
```

Keith also noticed all the people being weird. She smiled.

KEITH

```
Crazy.
```

They were fans. People who had come to see us. Some had already walked up to Frankie, who was holding his megaphone. They shook his hand and took pictures of him. Some had even brought the newspaper article and asked him to sign it.

And more people came. And more people. And more. Until it seemed like half the station was full with people, some young, some old, some black, some white, some Spanish, a few Asians, some obvious uptowners, some obvious downtowners, tattoos, dreadlocks, fedoras, suits, *everybody.* This was really happening.

I sat on my crate and lined my buckets up in front of me. I banged on a few just to get the sound and see what the acoustics were like at 125th. Not as good as Fourteenth Street, but still not bad. Lots of people had their phones out, already taking pictures.

Dunks turned around and looked at me. He bugged his eyes out and bit down on his fist like he couldn't believe what was happening. Keith looked the same way as she blew spit from her horn. Alexis too. He couldn't help but be excited about all these people here to see us play music. This was a dream come true. And we were still just beginning.

Frankie tested the megaphone. It screeched as he began to speak into it.

FRANKIE

`How many of y'all here to see Soundtrack?`

The crowd clapped and hooted.

FRANKIE

`Okay, okay, how many of y'all saw us in the newspaper?`

Dozens of people held their papers up, waving them around like they were some sort of concert souvenir.

FRANKIE

`Nice.`

Frankie nodded, then turned around to check on where we were as far as the whole setup. Dunks was still tuning his guitar. New strings.

FRANKIE

Well, I go by the name of Famous Frankie, and before we get started, we'd like to see who's here.

Frankie was confident. It's like no matter what, he just came alive whenever he had that megaphone. He started his usual roll call.

FRANKIE

Is Queens underground?

I stood up to see if I could spot Ashley. I mean, I didn't have a clue what she looked like.

FRANKIE

Bronx?

I probably could've just googled her like she did me, but I didn't. I don't really know why. I just didn't.

FRANKIE

What about Harlem?

I scanned the crowd, hoping that I would see someone who I just knew was related to me. I don't know, I guess I just figured family was family no matter what, and you could always recognize family. I looked and looked, but didn't see anyone who I thought could be her. I figured maybe she couldn't make it.

Maybe she just changed her mind. I could understand that. But I did see Dylan.

SG

```
Dylan!
```

She stood in the mix, bopping up and down. She threw her hand up and gave me an awkward wave. I called her up to where we were, and waited while she pushed through, excusing herself until finally she was free from the mob.

SG

```
Hey.
```

I gave her a hug.

DYLAN

```
Did I do okay?
```

Dylan was pulling her hair back behind her ear, just as Frankie was asking the crowd if any of them had seen us down at Fourteenth Street. About half the crowd roared.

SG

```
Yeah, homie. You did great. Thank you so
much!
```

She smiled and was headed back to the crowd when I pulled her back.

SG

```
You're with us.
```

DYLAN

Really?

Keith was standing on the other side of me. She leaned over and held her hand out.

KEITH

Hell, yeah. Stuy, you ready?

I nodded.

SG

Dunks!

He looked back at me and nodded. I turned to Alexis, who didn't look worried at all. He sat there with bass up on his stomach, looking cool as ever. Seeing him that way let me know right then and there that we were gonna rock it.

SG

Alexis!

He turned to me slowly, his lips curling into a grin.

SG

It's on you.

He nodded and turned back to the crowd. Frankie looked for the signal. Keith gave it. It was time.

FRANKIE

Everybody gather round! Come grab hold
of a brand-new sound!

And bigger than ever, with a bunch of people with us, we screamed, "We! Are! Soundtrack!"

In my mind, everything faded to black, except a spotlight that was on Alexis.

The big man stepped forward and ran his hand from the bottom of the neck of his bass to the top, and then went straight into a funky soul groove, like a Motown bass line, which let us know where we were taking it. I mean, we were in Harlem. Just seemed like the right thing to do, to pay tribute with a soundtrack for the history of the neighborhood.

I came in behind him with the rhythm. Keith bobbed her head, listening, waiting for the music to let her in. Dunks strummed the guitar, moving with more soul than I had ever seen him move with. Usually the dude was off-beat, looking like he was having a stroke. Not this time. He was smooth, his hand flicking the strings effortlessly as he strutted around like a star. Keith finally jumped in with us, playing a smooth horn rhythm over it all. It was like the trumpet was the voice for the music, and Keith had it singing the hell out this jam.

The crowd swayed back and forth, and almost everyone had their phones out, taping us. Frankie came back to the front, grooving. He put the megaphone to his mouth.

FRANKIE

Harlem, let me see you put your hands together. Like this.

Frankie put the megaphone down and began to clap. Frankie had them going, everybody laughing and clapping and stomping, and before you knew it, Famous Frankie had some old lady out in front of everybody trying to show him how to do old dances. It was amazing.

She would yell out something, but nobody could hear her. Then Frankie would put the megaphone up to her mouth, and she'd repeat herself.

OLD LADY

Y'all don't know nothing about the Watusi!

And she was right. Nobody knew anything about a Watusi. Or the Hitch Hike. Or the Tighten Up. But she was teaching Frankie and everybody else how to do them all. It was like we had taken this old lady back to a different place, like she had time-traveled to when she was our age, moving through a different Harlem. All because of the music. She turned our soul jam into an all-out dance party.

OLD LADY

This one's called the Mashed Potata!

As we played on and on, I kept leaning over to the left and to the right to see if I could spot my sister. There was so much happening with all the dancing that it would've been hard to tell if she was there or not. But I kept looking.

And finally, as sweat poured off me, as my arms literally felt like they were going to fall off, I saw her. Well, at least who I thought was her. No, actually, I knew it was her. She looked just like me.

She had slid her way to the front and had her arm around another young girl, and they were laughing and bopping around, but she wouldn't take her eyes off me. I flashed a smile. She flashed one back, and suddenly I wasn't so tired anymore. I was ready to play for another hour if the band was up for it. But as I leaned up, I saw someone I didn't want to see out of the corner of my eye.

No, not my mother. That actually wouldn't have been so bad.

But a police officer.

And those guys were like mice. If you saw one, you knew there was always another one close by. And there was. Two more. They started stepping forward, and then Alexis noticed them and instantly stopped playing.

One thing that's always the case with music is that when the bass drops out of a song, it empties the entire song out. Makes it hollow. And as soon as Alexis stopped, Keith pulled her lips away from the horn, also noticing the boys in blue. Then I stopped. Dunks played a few more licks before realizing that this wasn't a solo. He turned and saw the cops and stopped playing right away.

Keith pulled Frankie back. The crowd was confused and started looking around, wondering what was going on. Once they saw the police, I guess at first they figured the cops had come to shut the music down because we didn't have a permit, or we were playing too loud, too late, or something silly like that.

They didn't know that the cops were looking for Alexis, so the people broke out in boos, many dishing out thumbs-down. But when they saw the cops slowly put their hands on their beatdown sticks, everybody knew that they were here to collect somebody and backed off a little.

Instincts kicked in. At least for Keith, like she flashed back to the time they got caught in the music store tagging the CD cases. She motioned for Frankie to stay put, as she stepped up toward Alexis. He looked uncertain. He looked like he was thinking of running.

But he knew that would be a bad idea because if he did, there was a chance they would shoot him in the back—a good chance—or chase him down and give him a beating so bad that his deaf parents would be able to hear the screams—an even better chance. But the chance of him running and actually getting away? Almost impossible.

Alexis knew that. Keith knew it too and could tell that Alexis was thinking about it anyway. So when the cops took one more step forward and started with the whole "Is your name Alexis Brown?" bullshit, Keith stepped in front of him. Like a soldier. Like a mother.

The cops said something slick like:

OFFICER

Sweetheart, please get out of the way.

But it didn't matter because by the time their cocky grins showed up on their faces, underestimating Keith, Dunks had already stepped up and stood next to her. Now the three cops were a bit more frustrated, especially since all the people who were there to see us play—our audience, our fans—started to boo again, this time way louder than they did when the cops had first shown up. Frankie ran up next to Keith. She put her arm around him, sort of protecting him too in the midst of all the madness.

And last was me. I didn't wait until the end because I was scared. I mean, I was scared, though. But I waited because I just wasn't sure what was going to happen, and my mind was torn between my friend Alexis—my brother Alexis—and my sister Ashley, my new sister, who was staring at me in the crowd, her hand covering her open mouth. Her eyes looked worried. For me.

For all of us.

But when the rest of the band stepped up for Alexis, I felt like my sister needed to know that these people were my siblings too. I just prayed that her first time seeing me wouldn't have to end with my face smashed on the floor of the nasty train platform, cuffs being slapped on my wrists.

I stepped up and stood beside Dunks, looking down the line

at the band. Keith's chest was heaving, her eyes wet, but no tears had fallen. Dunks stood confident. Strong. Different than normal. It was that same random burst of moxie he showed when we first had the talk about whether or not Alexis and Keith were going to join the band. And I just stood there, with my sticks in my hand, which looking back on it all was a terrible idea.

The crowd now roared. I mean, they really barked at the police, who now were all prepared for some kind of war. We weren't there to fight. We were just there to stand. To block them from taking what we love. Especially knowing that the decision that Alexis made was to protect someone else. Now he needed protecting. And we were going to do just that.

Us, and all of them—our fans. Remember, this is Harlem, 125th Street. We were five black kids in a standoff with the cops. At this point, everyone was yelling, heckling the police.

CROWD

Leave 'em alone!
Ain't y'all got some real criminals to catch?
Oink, oink!

People had their phones out, taping everything the cops did. It was just something we did every time we saw police dealing with black kids. We taped them.

I looked back at Alexis. He looked scared. I looked at Ashley. She looked scared. I looked at Keith. She was still holding back the tears. Her chin was high, her lips tight. The cops tried to calm the crowd, but the crowd only got louder. And madder.

And it wasn't even because they hated cops so much. It was because they loved us.

But the cops couldn't feel that love. And they had a job to do.

They took another step forward. Hands on clubs. Another

step. Another. Billy clubs pulled from holsters. Another. Jesus Christ. Walkie-talkie.

POLICE OFFICER

We need backup. We need backup.

Camera flashes. God. God!

ALEXIS

Okay! Okay, okay!

He threw his hands up. We were a step or two away from something bad. Something bloody. The crowd volumed down. Alexis unstrapped his bass. Laid it on the ground.

ALEXIS

Okay, I'll go.

Alexis squeezed between Dunks and Keith slowly, his hands still high in the air. Everyone still had their cameras out, which was probably the only reason the cops didn't slam him to the ground, y'know, break a rib because of the inconvenience.

Alexis turned around, and one of the stocky cops slapped the cuffs on him, read him his rights, then walked the giant away.

POLICE OFFICER

You have the right to remain silent. Anything you say can and will be used against you in a court of law . . .

CHAPTER 15

I KNOW FOR A FACT THAT THIS WAS THE LONGEST NIGHT of my life. Hands down. But even though I know that, it was also such a blur. I mean, after Alexis was escorted out by the cops, the crowd slowly faded, people unsure of what to say to us since nobody really knew what was going on. People just kind of dropped their money in the case and snuck off. Everyone except Ashley. She hung around with her friend for as long she could before having to jet too. But we got a chance to at least meet.

SG

Ashley?

She smiled and held her hand out. I took it, shook it.

ASHLEY

I, uh, I'm sorry about what happened to your friend.

SG

It's okay.

Not really.

ASHLEY

```
You guys were awesome, though.
```

I examined her face. My nose. My chin. My teeth. None of which looked like my mother's, so these must've been my dad—our dad's—features. Crazy.

SG

```
Yeah, thanks.
```

I looked over my shoulder at Keith, Dunks, and Frankie.

SG

```
Listen, there's a lot going on.
```

ASHLEY

```
Yeah, yeah. Here, let me get your
number. I gotta get home anyway
before my mom changes the locks on
the door.
```

She smirked and rolled her eyes. She sounded annoyed by her mother. Something else we had in common.

We exchanged numbers, and she took off. Not the way I planned for our first meeting to go. But I also didn't plan for me and my friends to damn near have a showdown with NYPD. Or to have my homeboy arrested.

Keith was wrapping Alexis's bass cords up. She had already carefully placed his guitar in its case and snapped it shut. She cared for it as if it was her own. Dunks did his usual breakdown. Frankie helped to gather my buckets and things while I was speaking to Ashley. The silence between us made it seem hard to breathe. Thick like smoke.

SG

So, we going down there?

Keith didn't say anything. She just kept cleaning up Alexis's stuff. She wouldn't even look up.

DUNKS

Go where?

SG

To the precinct.

It seemed like the only thing we could do. I mean, either we went home and tried to sleep knowing Alexis was in jail, or we went to the precinct. I didn't necessarily know what we would do there, but at least we would be doing something.

KEITH

The precinct? For what, Stuy? Huh? For us to see him locked up like he some kind of animal?

Her voice was full of bite, and it seemed like it was aimed at me.

SG

I'm just saying.

KEITH

What are you saying, Stuy? Huh? I mean, this whole shit is because he was trying to protect *you*! He was trying to look out for *your* mother. If only you wasn't such a pussy and had the heart to do it yourself, he wouldn't be in there!

SG

Hey! I didn't ask him to do that.

KEITH

You didn't tell him not to either.

Keith moved closer to me, her fists balled tight.

FRANKIE

Chill!

DUNKS

Yeah, all this blaming ain't gonna solve nothing. Let's just try to figure out what we're gonna do.

Keith glared at me before finally backing off. I can't front, she had me shook a little.

Frankie went back to counting the money. He organized the bills—and it was a helluva lot—and had the coins all spread out on the ground, sifting through them, putting the quarters with the quarters, the dimes with dimes.

SG

Like I said, we should just go to the precinct. And see if we can bail him out.

Frankie looked up as he thumbed through the dollars, counting quietly, his mouth moving with each flick.

DUNKS

Wait.

Dunks was putting the pieces of the puzzle together.

DUNKS

You mean with . . .

SG

Yeah, with the studio money.

Keith's face softened up finally. I looked her in the eyes, the water still just sitting on the edge.

SG

Look, it's worth a shot. You down with that?

It was a good idea. At least it seemed like one. We didn't have all the money with us, but had they just told us how much it was going to be, I would've just shot back home, grabbed the rest, and shot back to Harlem and got him out. No sweat.

But what we didn't know was that we couldn't bail him out, because there wasn't a bail set. When you get arrested, you gotta go before a judge, and then he has to tell you how much you have to pay to get out on bail. But because Alexis had been arrested so late at night, on a Friday, his bail wouldn't be set until Monday.

JAIL CLERK

That's how it works.

The clerk looked at us like we were babies. Like we were stupid.

JAIL CLERK

```
So come on back down here on Monday
afternoon if you wanna try to get him out.
```

The thought of him being in a cage all weekend crushed us.

KEITH

```
Can we at least see him?
```

The clerk yucked, as if Keith had cracked some kind of joke. Like something was really funny.

JAIL CLERK

```
Can you see him? That's cute.
```

She turned her face back toward her computer. I guess that was our cue to leave, since to this lady, we had already disappeared.

CHAPTER 16

WHEN YOU HAVE A FRIEND LOCKED UP, THE EASIEST THING to do is come up with ideas about how to get him free. Trying to bail him out was probably the best idea we had, but definitely not the only one. The rest of them were bad, though. I mean, *really* bad.

DUNKS

```
We could just bust him out.
```

Dunks was looking at me with the straightest face ever.

SG

```
No. We can't.
```

Dunks sat on a fire hydrant and kept adjusting himself, trying to get comfortable, which was scientifically impossible.

DUNKS

```
We could just set up our gear and stuff
right here, outside the precinct, and
play the loudest, noisiest mess we can
```

think of until the cops have no choice but to let him out.

I leaned against the brick wall of the police station, my head pounding as if Alexis was trapped up there instead, banging his fists on the side of my brain trying to bust out.

Harlem was buzzing with people. Like I said, it was Friday night, so everybody was out. Drunk dates stumbled down the street, hands in the air trying to hail a yellow cab. Cool kid skaters, carrying their boards, because they were too cool to actually skate. Pretty girls around our age, sitting outside talking to boys about nothing, and if something, nothing good. And lights everywhere.

SG

Or they could just come out here and lock us up for disturbing the peace or whatever.

Dunks humphed, then stood up, another idea on the tip of his tongue.

DUNKS

But what if that's what we want? They come and arrest us and throw us in jail with Alexis. At least then he wouldn't be alone.

Dunks nodded, proud of what he had just come up with. And to be honest, part of me thought this was a really cool thing to say and was kind of brilliant in a dumb way.

But another part of me wished that Keith hadn't left to take

Frankie home so that she could've toasted Dunks's ass for that one. But then again, as much as Keith loved Alexis, she might've thought this was a good plan too. So maybe it was better that she was gone.

SG

Look, man, I got an idea.

Now, I wasn't sure if this idea was actually a good idea, but it was definitely better than the ones Dunks had been shooting at me. And it came from what Keith had said to me when she was jumping down my throat about how it was my fault Alexis was in there. She was calling me a punk for letting Alexis go to my house to scare Dummy. For not doing it myself. So . . .

SG

I'm going home.

Dunks instantly started grabbing his guitar and all his stuff to come with me.

SG

No, I mean, I'm going *home* . . . to Brooklyn.

Dunks stopped.

DUNKS

Oh. Well, still, I'll come with you.

He continued gathering his crap. I grabbed the pushcart with the buckets in it.

SG

```
No. Go home. I need to do this alone.
```

We glared at each other, and I could tell I was looking in the face of Dunks the human, not Dunks the alien. I knew he understood me. He nodded, then he reached out for the pushcart full of buckets and pans.

DUNKS

```
I'll take this. I'm taking a cab anyway,
man.
```

I took the train. I knew it seemed dumb for Dunks to take a cab and for me to take the train, but if you looked like me, and it was late, and you were going to Brooklyn, you were pretty much cab kryptonite. The messed-up part was that I intended to go straight to Brooklyn, but forgot that I needed to stop at Uncle Lucky's first, so I actually could've just jumped in a cab with Dunks since we ended up going to the same place.

I snuck inside Uncle Lucky's, doing everything I could to not let Dunks know that I was there. I didn't want any questions. Not yet. I reached under the couch, way back, and pulled the old shoebox forward.

The money—all the money that we had saved for the past few months—was bundled in rubber bands. I grabbed the wads and threw them into my backpack, put the backpack on backward so that I was wearing it on my front to keep an eye and a hand on the money, then headed back out for Brooklyn.

Like a ninja.

Once I got off the train in my old neighborhood, I walked quickly, one hand in my pocket and one hand out. It was a trick my mother taught me when I was young.

STUY'S MOM

```
One hand in, one hand out. That way, if
anybody is thinking about robbing you,
they have to question why you only have
one hand in your pocket, and what that
hand may be holding.
```

Even though I looked ridiculous with this backpack strapped to my chest, making me waddle like a pregnant lady, I still kept one hand in my pocket, one hand out. It was a trick that really worked better in the winter, because it made stickup kids ask, "If he's not cold enough to put both hands in his pockets, what might that other hand be holding?" It wasn't cold, but I did it anyway. Habit.

I sped down the weirdly quiet street, stepping around canners—people who dig through everybody's trash in the middle of the night looking for cans and bottles to sell for money—and the neighborhood junkies, like Roxanne, a woman who you could tell used to be pretty when she was younger. Well, I didn't really know if she was old or young, but she definitely looked old. She might've been twenty-one for all I knew and just smoked herself old. She was out there, pacing back and forth, moving her hands like she was shuffling an imaginary deck of cards. When I passed her, she waved to me and mumbled something. I pretended I didn't see her and kept moving.

My block. Dark. Quiet. Nothing like Harlem. Trash cans set outside of every house ready for trash pickup. A random bed frame. A girl walking up the block toward me. She had on sweatpants. One hand in, one hand out.

278 Hancock. Home. I walked the stoop slowly, sluggishly, thinking, *I hope this asshole didn't change the locks.* Wouldn't have surprised me if my mother let him. I flipped through my key

ring, the copper drumstick key chain getting in the way. Then I slipped the key in, turn, click.

One more door to go. This was the tricky part. I didn't want to just go in, even though I could've. But Dummy was crazy, and if I went in there without them knowing I was coming, in the middle of the night, it was almost a guarantee that something crazy would happen.

So I decided to bang on the door. I know, not really a bright idea either. But it was the best I had. At least the door would be between Dummy and me, and he could hear my voice before he opened the door to know I wasn't some weird jack boy who liked to knock on the door before he robbed people.

I banged and banged until finally, I could hear him cursing on the other side of the wood. He unlocked everything except for the chain lock. Then he cracked the door and peered through the opening, his bloodshot eye—the eye I could see—going from a wide circle to a thin straight line as he realized it was me.

DOM

Whatchu want?

My heart was pounding. Looking at Dummy was like staring into the face of an angry dog.

SG

To talk.

To the point. Don't let him see your fear. One hand in, one hand out.

DOM

About *what*?

STUY'S MOM

Who's that?

My mother's voice came from behind him.

DOM

Nobody. Go back to the room and let me handle this.

SG

It's me, Ma.

STUY'S MOM

Stuy?

Her voice, sweet as usual. Even when she was half asleep, she sounded like an angel.

SG

I just want to talk.

He didn't say anything. He just closed the door. I put my ear to the cold wood and could hear my mother asking him to let me in. Practically begging him. It made me cringe to hear her pleading with this dude. Like he was her boss. Her master. This was her house! I was her son! Then, the sound of the chain sliding. The knob turning. The door cracking open again.

My mother pulled the door the rest of the way and stood there in her nightgown, tattoos all up and down her arms, concern painted across her face.

STUY'S MOM

Baby.

She sounded a little worried but still opened her arms to me.

I gave her a hug, but it wasn't a full one. Just something to let her know I loved her, but that we weren't okay. As long as my homeboy was in jail and she was still with this lunatic, we were *not* okay.

SG

```
I just need to talk . . . to him.
```

I slid past her. Dummy sat at the kitchen table in his underwear. The hair on his chest rolled up into tiny black pebbles, and his body, though big, was loose. The left side of his face was covered by gauze, black and blue peeking from the edges. Alexis really did a job on him. Looked painful.

The house looked different. I couldn't put my finger on what it was, but in the few months I had been gone, things had definitely changed.

The sink dripped.

DOM

```
You need to talk to me, huh?
```

I pulled a chair out from the table, took a seat, and looked at him square.

SG

```
Yeah. I need you to get my friend out of jail.
```

He flashed an evil grin and shook his head. And while placing both of his hands on the top of his head, he simply said:

DOM

```
No.
```

SG

He's only eighteen.

DOM

Ah.

That smile again.

DOM

See, what he is is an attacker.
And an adult.

SG

What he is is a defender. And a hero.

DOM

And who was he defending?

SG

You know exactly who he was defending.

I glanced at my mother, who was leaning against the refrigerator, her eyes to the floor. The sink dripped.

DOM

Let me explain something to you, son, and
I want you to hear me and hear me good.

Dummy scooted his chair into the table and leaned in as close as he could. Close enough for me to smell the sleep funk on his breath.

DOM

```
What happens in my house with my woman
is my business. You understand?
```

I squeezed my hand into a fist, digging my nails into my palm, and bit down on the inside of my jaw. Every time he said "my," I felt a shock in my gut. There was so much I wanted to say. There was so much I wanted to do, like jump across the table and try to put my fist through the other side of his face. I wasn't really that kinda guy, but at that moment, something was alive in me, something vicious. And all I wanted to do was let it out. Turn that slick smile to mush.

The sink dripped.

SG

```
Man, what will it take? To drop the
charges. What will it take?
```

STUY'S MOM

```
Dom.
```

Dummy's laughter stopped short, and he shot a laser glare at my mother. I rocked up on my toes just in case this asshole decided he wanted to show me what he does to her when I'm not around. Not this time. No way.

DOM

```
What?
```

He turned his whole body so that he could see her out of his good eye.

My mother looked at him, fear sitting on the edges of her eyes, ready to roll down. She opened her mouth but decided to eat her words and save herself the problems. Even with double the vision, she was afraid of him.

He turned back toward me.

DOM

Okay, Stuy. What would you suggest is a good deal? Maybe you let me hit you, huh? You let me get a clean shot. What you think about that?

SG

How about I pay you the money to cover some of your doctor bills?

I leaned back. I pointed at his eye. Dummy was shocked and matched me by leaning back in his chair too.

DOM

Stuy, Stuy, Stuy. You don't have that kind of money.

I sat there for a second, staring at a man that I was sure that I hated. I don't think I had ever hated anyone before, but I knew for a fact I hated him. But I wanted Alexis out of jail. I owed it to him. I also wanted my mom to leave this dude, but that didn't seem like it was happening anytime soon.

I stood up, unzipped the front pouch of my backpack, and threw the cash knots on the table. They thumped like bricks.

SG

That's about three thousand dollars.

I folded my arms in front of me. Dummy looked at the money on the table like it was something else. Like it was a time bomb. Like he was scared to touch it.

DOM

Where'd you get this?

SG

Music.

I nodded at the newspaper clip my mother had stuck to the fridge by a magnet that said ROCK ON. Alexis's face was scribbled over with a pen. Dummy was such a loser.

I repeated it, now staring at my mother:

SG

Music.

She wiped her eyes before any water came out but couldn't stop the sniffles. Again, she wanted to say something, even opened her mouth to, but only breath came out. She talked to Uncle Lucky almost every day, so I knew she knew what that money was for. She knew that we were working to save up to record an album, to get into a real studio and do it the right way. She knew this was a sacrifice, and that as much as I was paying to get him to drop Alexis's charges, I was also hoping this money could bring her back to reality. Back to being awesome, without this man. This wasn't happiness. He never deserved to see that dress that zipped up the back.

SG

Please drop the charges. *Please.*

I watched Dummy flip through the bills. Then I grabbed my bag and headed for the door.

STUY'S MOM

Stuy.

I didn't answer her. I had nothing else to say.

Again, the sink dripped.

IN THE MORNING—ALEXIS'S LOCKUP day number one—I was awakened by my uncle, who was sitting on the couch. On me. Like I wasn't trying to sleep. He slurped down a cup of coffee, ate cereal, and watched cartoons like some kind of adult-child. He pretended like he didn't know he was crushing my legs, until finally he turned toward me and acted like he was surprised to see me lying there.

UNCLE LUCKY

Oh, good morning, nephew.

SG

Unc, what are you doing?

He lifted up long enough for me to slide my legs out from under him. I curled into a tight ball at the other end of the couch.

UNCLE LUCKY

I'm just not used to ever seeing you. During the week, I'm working, and you're running around with the rest of the Little Rascals, and on Saturdays when I'm not working, you're usually . . . running around with the Little Rascals.

I yawned and scooted up until I was sitting at ninety degrees. I stretched my arms above my head and felt the new day trickle down my back and legs.

SG

Long night. I'm chillin' today.

UNCLE LUCKY

Yeah, I heard you come in.

He reached for his cereal.

UNCLE LUCKY

What, y'all played ten encores, superstar?

I looked at the TV. Didn't recognize the characters. I couldn't even remember the last time I had watched a cartoon.

SG

Man, I wish. The cops found Alexis last night.

Unc put his bowl back on the table and turned the TV down.

UNCLE LUCKY

Your boy?

SG

Yep.

UNCLE LUCKY

How?

SG

Who knows. Somebody probably was passing the word about us playing there and passed it to the wrong person. One person knew another person, who knew a cop that was on the case. Probably something like that.

UNCLE LUCKY

Wow. Bad luck.

SG

Tell me about it. They took him down to the precinct. We went down there and tried to get him out, but they said he had to stay through the weekend. So I went to see Dummy.

Now Uncle Lucky's eyes got wide enough to burst.

UNCLE LUCKY

You did *what*?

SG

I went to talk to him, man to man.

It felt good saying that, man to man.

Uncle Lucky grabbed his coffee and stood up. I didn't know what it was about sitting on a couch talking to someone that you always felt like you had to stand up whenever you thought there was big news about to drop.

UNCLE LUCKY

```
And?
```

SG

```
And I did what I had to do.
```

My uncle looked at me, frustrated. I could tell he thought I had done something stupid.

UNCLE LUCKY

```
Which was?
```

SG

```
Relax. I offered to pay his medical bills
in exchange for him dropping the charges.
```

UNCLE LUCKY

```
You offered to pay his medical bills?
```

Uncle Lucky really looked confused now.

SG

```
Yeah. Three grand that the band raised
for the studio.
```

Uncle Lucky became a ghost. He looked so concerned, so afraid, as if I had told him that I did something stupid. But I didn't. Did I?

Uncle Lucky plopped back down on the couch, all huffy.

SG

What?

I was a little worried. He was freaking me out.

UNCLE LUCKY

Kid, tell me you didn't already give him the money.

Instantly, an alarm inside me went off that was connected to a time bomb. The explosion rumbled in my stomach and crept up my throat.

SG

Yeah, I did.

UNCLE LUCKY

Damn it, Stuy. Damn it, damn it, damn it. You know you just gave that money away, right? You know that, right?

At the time, I didn't know that. But sitting on the couch talking to my uncle . . . yes, I knew that I had just gotten got.

SG

I mean, maybe he'll stick to his word.

My uncle snorted, then reached for his cereal. The milk had turned pink and green and yellow, and colorful Os floated around like buoys. He scooped as many as he could onto his spoon.

UNCLE LUCKY

Yeah, Stuy, maybe. But let me tell you

```
something—don't come crying to me about
getting your money back from him when
he spends it on whatever that fool
likes to spend his money on, because I
can't help you.
```

SG

```
I know. If that does happen, we'll just
figure out how to make more.
```

UNCLE LUCKY

```
Yeah, just remember that your bass
player is in jail, and you done spent up
all the bail money already.
```

Ah. Uncle Lucky was right. If Dummy decided to run with the cash, it would take us a long time to make it back because we're short our bass player. We made that money as a band. All of us together. Without Alexis, the music wouldn't be the same. But without money, we wouldn't be able to bail Alexis out if Dummy decided to be . . . Dummy.

SG

```
I was just trying to make it right.
```

I felt like a stone-cold fool.

UNCLE LUCKY

```
I know you were, nephew. Ain't nothing
you can do it about it now but wait.
```

Uncle Lucky looked sorry for me, even though he was chewing hard, like cereal was meat or something. He turned the bowl up to his face and slurped down the milk. Then, wiping the milk off his mouth, he said:

UNCLE LUCKY

Now, man to man, since you got some time on your hands, wash up and come with me down to the laundromat.

Seriously, who only washes clothes once a month? Uncle Lucky, that's who. I never really had to do all this because when I showed up to my uncle's apartment that first night, I only had a backpack with me. All the clothes that I needed were in there. I washed them in the sink every other day to keep them fresh. But this dude literally waited until he didn't have anything else to wear before he decided to wash.

SG

Man to man, you gotta do better than this, Unc.

I lugged the big bag down the block, trying not to let it hit the ground because laundry bags rip easily, and there's nothing worse than having to run back down the street to get a random sock that escaped.

SG

This thing is like a hundred pounds!

UNCLE LUCKY

Hey, nephew, tell me something. Are you gonna cry like this the whole way?

He was ahead of me and looked over his shoulder while continuing:

UNCLE LUCKY

When me and your mother were kids, we used to have to do everybody's laundry. Mine, hers, our parents. Sometimes neighbors. And we couldn't get none of it mixed up either.

SG

Yeah, but all of those clothes probably equaled half of what you got!

UNCLE LUCKY

Oh, so you *are* gonna cry like this the whole way.

He hiked the bag up on his shoulder.

UNCLE LUCKY

Lord, give me the strength. Matter fact, Lord give my weak-ass nephew strength.

Of course, the laundromat was crowded. It was Saturday, everybody's wash day. The smell of bleach, fabric softener, and mildew funk was just as good a welcome as the drop-off girl's. Her name was Debbie. All she said when we came in was:

DEBBIE

Droppin' off?

With a face that said: I hope your ass ain't droppin' all that mess off.

And when we told her that we weren't, she just dropped her head and went right back to folding someone's tighty-whities.

We dumped the clothes into a few different machines. The whites in one, the colors in another. Towels and sheets in another. Uncle Lucky went down the line popping in quarters and pouring in the detergent, the blue green slime turning the water into soap instantly.

People were carefully scooting past each other, and the dryers were kicking out so much heat that it was impossible to just sit in there and watch whatever boring Saturday-morning program Debbie had on the TV. So we went outside.

A car pulled up. A man jumped out and ran into the laundromat. A few seconds later, he came hustling out with a bag of fresh washed and folded clothes. He threw them in the trunk, jumped back behind the wheel, turned his music up, and sped off.

UNCLE LUCKY

You see your mother when you were over there last night?

I didn't really want to talk about all that anymore.

SG

Yeah. She the only reason he even let me in.

My uncle cracked his knuckles, then massaged his hands.

UNCLE LUCKY

How she doin'?

SG

She seem to be doin' alright. Hard to tell, though. I hate that dude.

UNCLE LUCKY

I know you do. You have every reason to. But you hating him ain't gonna make your mother leave him. That's her decision.

He was right. But it felt good to hate him, and even though Uncle Lucky didn't say it, I knew he hated Dummy too. He was just trying to be all deep.

UNCLE LUCKY

Man, if it was up to me, I would've gone back to the old Lucky. Crazy Lucky.

He smiled at the thought before glancing at me.

UNCLE LUCKY

But your mom is a big girl. She ain't my little sister banging on her drums anymore.

A woman walked up, pushing a cart full clothes. She wore neon green tights and a wrinkled T-shirt. A laundry day outfit. Her hair was pulled back in a bun, and huge sunglasses covered most of her face.

LISA

Hey, Lucky, where you been hiding?

He leaned in and gave her a hug and a kiss on the cheek.

UNCLE LUCKY

Lisa, I've been chillin', looking out for my nephew here.

The lady turned to me with her hand out.

SG

Stuy.

LISA

Lisa.

UNCLE LUCKY

You good?

LISA

Yeah, I'm good. Getting ready to do these clothes.

She nodded to the overflowing cart.

UNCLE LUCKY

You wanna knock mine out while you in there?

He winked so smoothly that I almost didn't even see it.

LISA

Boy, please!

She laughed and slapped him on the chest.

LISA

Look. You just call me when you free. Maybe by then we'll both have clean clothes to wear out.

She flirted perfectly, and Unc was right there to throw it back. I was just taking notes.

UNCLE LUCKY

`How you just gonna invite yourself out on a date with me? That ain't the way this goes.`

LISA

`Yeah, but it's the way that it is. So . . .`

She flashed a sexy smirk. Then she turned to me.

LISA

`Nice to meet you, baby.`

She stepped into laundry madness. Uncle Lucky watched her walk in. Like, he really, really watched her walk in. Then he finally snapped out of it.

UNCLE LUCKY

`Yeah, like I was saying, your mother ain't my baby sister no more, that's for sure.`

SG

`Naw, wait, who was that?`

Uncle Lucky lightly jabbed me in the shoulder.

UNCLE LUCKY

`None of your business. Just know that`

Crazy Lucky ain't all the way dead. He a little less crazy, but he still around.

Uncle Lucky took one last look at Lisa.

UNCLE LUCKY

But back to your mother. Look, the only thing that she's ever loved more than music is *you*. When you came, she didn't really play much anymore because she was focused on taking care of *you*, but she did everything she could to give you music. You used to bang on everything, just like her.

Uncle Lucky checked his watch.

UNCLE LUCKY

When did we put the clothes in?

SG

Like ten minutes ago.

UNCLE LUCKY

Okay.

An older lady came out of the laundromat and told us to have a blessed day.

UNCLE LUCKY

You do the same. Now, the only thing your mother wanted to give you, besides music, was a family.

SG

A family? I have a family.

UNCLE LUCKY

Yeah, I know that. But she wanted to give you a *perfect* family. She's always been that way. Our father died when we were young, so we didn't really have it. And even though we were fine, she always wanted it to be like it was on those cheesy shows we watched as kids. *Facts of Life*, and all that. That's why the Dusters was such a big deal. They were a whole thing. All the pieces were there. And that's why she took it hard when it fell apart, with them and with Bottom. So since then, it's been about creating that life for you. At least that's what I think. She wanted you to have a whole band. And by band, I mean a mother and a father.

SG

But I had you.

UNCLE LUCKY

And you see how that went. Let's face it, Stuy, I wasn't the greatest father figure.

SG

But you *did* teach me how to dial 911.

Uncle Lucky's shoulders bounced as he held his laugh in.

UNCLE LUCKY

That's for damn sure. But she wanted you guys to be like, I don't know, a *family* family. A unit. And I think that's what she was hoping Dom would be. The missing piece to the family puzzle.

No comment. Uncle Lucky checked his watch again.

UNCLE LUCKY

Come on. Let's load the dryers.

We flung the wet clothes into a few separate dryers, handfuls at a time. The lady at the dryer next to us watched her clothes go round and round. She looked hypnotized.

But really, she was just protecting her stuff. People are known for just opening up your dryer and walking off with a grip of your clothes like it's nothing. One time when I was a kid, my mother sent me to do the laundry. She gave me the same instructions she gave me every time—to watch the clothes. To not walk away. But of course, I put the clothes in, then ran across the street to the bodega to just get a juice with the quarters I had left. By the time I got back to the laundromat, half the load was gone.

And the crazy part was about a month later, we saw a woman walking up the block in a Bed-Stuy Magic Dusters shirt. My mother's shirt.

But my mom, being the peaceful woman she was, let it go and hit me with this whole nonsense:

STUY'S MOM

If she had to steal it, she needed it more than I did.

Uncle Lucky loaded the quarters and hit the START button on each machine. The spinning began, and so did the watching. And the sweating.

My phone buzzed in my pocket. I checked it, already knowing it was Dunks, wondering where I was.

1 NEW MESSAGE

ASHLEY:

everything cool?

It was Ashley!

rough night.

im sure. is your friend ok?

he's still in there. trying to figure out how to get him out

Buzz.

damn. let me know if i can help :/

thx, we will wrk it out. but we still need to hang. like forreal.

Buzz.

wassup with tmw?

tmw is perfect. just hit me in the morning

Buzz.

cool :)

I looked up from my phone expecting to find Uncle Lucky hypnotized by the spin cycle, but instead he was looking at Lisa, who was now a few dryers down from us, bent over loading her clothes.

SG

Unc. Unc!

UNCLE LUCKY

Yeah, yeah.

SG

I was trying to say something to you.

He ran his hand along his forehead to swipe the sweat. He seemed irritated that I had broken his concentration.

UNCLE LUCKY

So say it.

SG

I was just saying, speaking of missing pieces, I found out I have a sister.

It dawned on me that I hadn't told Uncle Lucky about Ashley at all. And this was a big deal. Major news!

UNCLE LUCKY

What you talking about?

Uncle Lucky placed his hand against the dryer door to make sure it was hot. Even though it was ten million degrees in the laundromat, that didn't mean that every dryer was hot. Sometimes the dryers got overworked and lost some of the heat. Next thing you knew, you were down five dollars and your clothes were still wet.

SG

Just what I said, Unc. I have a sister. Her name's Ashley.

UNCLE LUCKY

Ashley? Really?

SG

Really.

UNCLE LUCKY

I'm guessing on your daddy's side, 'cause I know my sister couldn't have slipped this one past me.

I laughed and put a hand on his shoulder.

SG

Yeah, man, Ashley is Bottom's daughter. Found out about her a few nights ago when I YouTubed Mom's old band. There's only one clip of a show they played at CBGB a long time ago. They were doing a song called "Rotten Apple." Know it?

An old man tried to push a quarter in one of the dryers and missed the slot. The coin clinked and tumbled right up to Uncle Lucky's foot.

UNCLE LUCKY

Stuy, I'll be honest.

He picked up the quarter for the old man.

OLD MAN

Thank you very much.

UNCLE LUCKY

I was never really into that whole scene. I mean, I loved your mother's playing, but I wasn't into punk. I was more interested in what LL Cool J was talking about.

SG

Well, this song is pretty dope. And to see my mother up there rocking out was wild. She had chops.

UNCLE LUCKY

Hell yeah, she did.

SG

But anyway, the person who posted this video I found out was Bottom's daughter, Ashley. My sister.

UNCLE LUCKY

Have you talked to her?

SG

We chatted online that night. And then

she came to our show last night, in Harlem, but because of all the drama, we really didn't get a chance to speak. But we're supposed to catch up tomorrow.

The theme song of one of those political talk shows that come on Saturday mornings played. Even the theme song sounded political. Marching drums and regal horns. Stiff, stiff, stiff. I preferred coming to the laundromat on weekdays, when you could at least catch a talk show. Or a game show. And even though those were stupid, they definitely helped the time go by much quicker.

UNCLE LUCKY

Say anything about your father?

SG

Just that he loved music more than anything.

UNCLE LUCKY

He's dead?

SG

Yeah. Recently. And the messed-up part, he'd been living in the Bronx pretty much this whole time.

Uncle Lucky's jaw dropped.

UNCLE LUCKY

You're kidding.

SG

```
My whole life.
```

I shook my head, still not really able to believe that. I wondered if he was still around, and we were cool, if he would have let Dummy put his hands on my mother. I imagined he wouldn't have. That I would've just called him, and he would've come right over and let Dummy know what time it was.

UNCLE LUCKY

```
You told your mother?
```

SG

```
No. Not yet.
```

UNCLE LUCKY

```
Wow.
```

Uncle Lucky shot his eyes toward the ceiling and tongued the inside of his cheek the way people did when they were thinking about something.

UNCLE LUCKY

```
Well, I wanna meet this Ashley.
```

SG

```
Tomorrow.
```

LATER THAT EVENING, I HIT up Keith to see if maybe her and Frankie wanted to come hang with me and Dunks. We weren't doing much besides moping around really and thought it might be a good idea to just hang out. No music. Maybe catch a movie or some food.

I hadn't told anybody about what I did with the money, and I wasn't going to until I was sure of whether Dummy was going to just keep it and not hold up his part of the deal or be a man of his word.

It's not that I was trying to lie to my crew, but . . . yeah, I just needed to keep this a secret. At least until I knew how it was going to play out, which I would know by Monday. Then I'd come clean.

Keith said that Frankie still wasn't feeling too hot and was spending the day in bed. And she was actually going to go by Alexis's house to hang out with his parents. By now, Keith figured Alexis's folks had gotten the phone call from him and were pretty upset. And if for some reason Alexis hadn't called them, Keith was going to tell them herself, just in case we couldn't get Alexis out of there and they were wondering where their son was spending his nights.

SG

You want me and Dunks to meet you over there?

KEITH

Naw. It's right around the corner from me. And they've known me pretty much my whole life. I got it.

So Dunks and I spent the night walking. Just walking. Our original intention was to head to the West Side to catch one of those independent movies. I always liked going to those theaters because they had way more variety when it came to snacks. You could get, like, dinner at some of these places. I'm talking burgers.

And Dunks was all about the fact that they were independent. He just felt like that made them better, because if they were indie, then the people who made them were probably, you guessed it, aliens.

But we never actually got to the theater. Instead we just walked and talked about stuff that Dunks and I never talked about, even though I was with him every day.

SG

Dude, when's the last time you spoke to your dad?

DUNKS

Man, I think the last time I heard from him was on my birthday. So, February.

SG

And what did he say?

DUNKS

Nothing. He sent me an email.

SG

Well, what did the email say?

Dunks looked at me, a glimpse of pain behind his eyes.

DUNKS

Happy birthday.

SG

That's it?

DUNKS

```
That's it.
```

A homeless man limped toward us. He was dressed in clothes that looked like he had been attacked by a lion. Everything was shredded, his dignity included. He shook a dirty coffee cup at people walking by, hoping that someone would drop a quarter or dime in to add to the jingling coins that he had already collected. When he got to us, he shook the cup in Dunks's face.

HOMELESS MAN

```
Man, you got some change?
```

Dunks being Dunks, he stuffed a few dollar bills in.

DUNKS

```
What about you? When you gonna tell your
mother about Ashley?
```

SG

```
No time soon. All I'm really thinking
about is Alexis. I mean, whether or not
I want anything to do with my mom has
everything to do with how this whole
thing turns out.
```

I knew that seemed like a harsh thing to say, but I meant it. It wasn't like I hated her or anything like that. I loved her. She was my mom. She gave me everything. But until I was able to give her what she deserved, I couldn't stand watching her take crap from some lame. She was better than that. And I was much better off not seeing her beg or act like she's not.

SG

```
What about your mom?
```

The day had faded to a dark blue, the lights of the cars and bicycle reflectors shooting all around us. The smoke in the air changed with every few steps, from cigarette, to halal meat, to exhaust pipes, to incense, all of which were like us, just floating along.

DUNKS

```
What about her?
```

SG

```
I mean, you never really say much
about her. I've never seen her or
anything.
```

It had been on my mind for a little while. I knew about Dunks's father and the bullshit he pulled on the family. Seemed like Lady Luck only liked scumbags. But Dunks never really mentioned his mom.

DUNKS

```
Man, my mom is at home. In the same
house I grew up in.
```

SG

```
Where's that?
```

Dunks looked at me, his eyes two fading moons.

DUNKS

```
Downstairs. Apartment 1A.
```

SG

What?! Next to Ms. Bednick?

DUNKS

Yep. Right next to Ms. Bednick.

SG

Well, why haven't I met her?

We were approaching Hudson Street. I could see the lights from the pier reflecting on the water.

DUNKS

Because.

He stopped walking in the middle of the sidewalk. So I stopped. A guy behind us almost slammed right into us because he was looking down at his cell phone.

GUY

Yo! Watch where you're going, man!

DUNKS

Because she never leaves the house. I go there early in the morning, and we have tea and listen to jazz. Sometimes I play acoustic guitar for her if she's in the mood. She writes me a list of the things she needs, and I take it to her. And that's it. By the time you wake up, her and I have already had our time.

I couldn't believe what I was hearing, but I knew I was hearing it right.

SG

```
But I don't understand. Why won't she
leave the apartment?
```

It was definitely an honest question, but way out of line. I knew that. But we were having such an honest conversation, it seemed like an okay thing to ask.

DUNKS

```
The golden question.
```

We were now standing off to the side, while the sidewalk traffic of runners, baby strollers, and fully dressed French bulldogs whizzed by us.

DUNKS

```
Man, I guess after my father disappeared,
he took some of her with him.
```

I didn't say anything. Didn't have anything else to say. Especially since I could kind of relate. Both of us wanting our moms to be okay. Hell, maybe I'm an alien too.

DUNKS

```
You know what I ask her every morning?
```

Dunks looked down the block.

SG

```
What?
```

DUNKS

If she would come see me play, because I know that would give her some life back, y'know? And you know what she says?

SG

What does she say?

DUNKS

She says "soon." Every morning she says "soon."

Dunks's eyes began to sparkle. The light from the streetlight was hitting the tears welling in his eyes from the perfect angle, like Dunks could cry diamonds at any moment.

DUNKS

But it never happens.

SG

It will. She will.

Then we turned and headed back the way we came.

CHAPTER 17

SUNDAY. ALEXIS'S LOCKUP DAY NUMBER TWO. WHILE A LOT of the city was doing their weekly religious rituals, I was doing one of my own—praying that this would be Alexis's last day in the slam and that somehow Dummy would be nice enough to drop the charges.

It was worth a shot. If it didn't happen, I was going to have to break it to the rest of the band that not only did Alexis go to jail for trying to protect my mom, but I also gave the man she needed protection from everything that we had worked for. Not a great conversation to have.

But it was going to have to happen if Alexis didn't come home tomorrow.

After that short prayer, which took place right there on the couch with a sheet over my head—bedside Baptist, as my mother used to call it—I got up and got myself together.

Uncle Lucky wasn't around. Who knows where he went, and who cares?

Not me, because today was the day I was going to hang out with Ashley. I wasn't sure where we were going to meet up. I just told her to hit me in the morning, and that's exactly what she did.

At like eight a.m. I didn't get it until around ten when I got up, but still . . . eight o'clock? She was already acting like a little sister. But it was cool, because at least I knew she was as excited as I was.

ASHLEY

where???

Those three question marks were like asking three times. The text really said, "WHERE? WHERE? WHERE?" Which translates to "HURRY UP AND ANSWER ME BECAUSE I'M HYPE!"

I texted back, now two hours after she sent the original message.

should i come uptwn?

naw. nothing to do up here.
i'll come dwntwn. what stop?

Awesome. I would've gone uptown to meet her, but I was so glad she volunteered to come down. Downtown was so much better most of the time, unless we were going to meet in Harlem. But even though I had been living in the Lower East Side, I was from Brooklyn, and you know, Brooklyn and Harlem were just . . . different.

sweet. come to delancey. call me when you get off.

Buzz.

I didn't get the call from her until two hours later. I was sitting across the hall in Dunks's apartment with Keith. She said Frankie was taking it easy, that his parents just wanted him to rest to kick whatever he had. Probably just a head cold, she said.

Me and Dunks sat back listening to Keith do her best impressions of Miles Davis and Louis Armstrong. And not on the horn either. Instead she was impersonating their voices.

KEITH

Okay, so Louis, right, his voice was kinda like the horn. It was raspy, kind of like he had a forever cold, but it was still musical, y'know?

She strutted around Dunks's living room singing "Hello, Dolly."

KEITH

But Miles . . . Miles's voice was so raspy that it just sounded like a whisper. Dude sounded like it hurt him to talk.

Keith looking over at Dunks and whispered:

KEITH

Hey, man.

She bopped over toward him. Dunks sat on the couch with his legs crossed at the ankles and his hands behind his head. No shirt, short shorts, dirty socks. When she got over to him, she said, still in her Miles Davis voice:

KEITH

Did the aliens come and steal the rest of your chest, birdie?

SG

Awwwww, man, Dunks. Don't let her get you like that.

KEITH

It wasn't me! It was Miles.

DUNKS

Well, Miles . . .

Dunks prepared for his comeback.

DUNKS

Maybe they did. Right after they took your voice.

KEITH

That's not funny, Dunks. That man really lost his voice. And he was a legend.

Dunks got scared and started backpedaling. Being the music head he was, one thing he never wanted to do was disrespect a great.

DUNKS

Okay, wait. I'm sorry. I'm sorry.

Keith glared at him as long as she could before erupting into laughter again.

KEITH

Jokes, Dunks. Just jokes!

She wrapped her arms around his neck, still laughing. It was good to see her being herself. All of us being ourselves.

After Ashley texted me that she had made it, I left, walked down to Delancey to get her, and when we got back to Dunks's, he and Keith were watching a clip of Miles Davis on YouTube. It was from 1989, when he was on the *Arsenio Hall Show.* His hair was long, jet black, and weirdly straight. It didn't even look like it belonged to him. He wore a multicolored, patchy jacket in that old-school swish-swish material, and baggy black pants.

Miles held his black trumpet to his mouth, and Keith held her hands up as if she was holding her horn, her fingers moving right along with Miles's. Keith knew every single note of the song "Jo-Jo" and was putting on an imaginary concert for Dunks, who was looking at her as if she was really playing with Miles.

Ashley and I didn't interrupt. We just came in and watched the rest of the performance. At the end, we clapped.

SG

Bravo!

I blew Keith kisses as she took fifteen bows. Dunks stood up and gave her a standing ovation as the YouTube clip ended.

ASHLEY

This is the episode where Miles talks about how he thinks Prince is a genius.

Keith made a face at me that let me know she was already impressed.

KEITH

Whoever this is, I like her.

Keith held her hand out to Ashley.

SG

Keith, Dunks, this is my little sister, Ashley. Ashley, this is Keith and Dunks.

Ashley shook their hands.

DUNKS

Sit anywhere.

KEITH

Don't be scared. It's dirty, but it ain't . . . well, you know what? I can't blame you if you're scared. This place is a mess.

Ashley plopped down on the floor and fell right into the groove. We watched a few more clips of Miles (because Keith was on a roll), then a few of Louis Armstrong, including "When the Saints Go Marching In," which me and Dunks knew was Keith's favorite.

ASHLEY

I got one.

Ashley spoke up after a few Louis clips, and Keith was clearly exhausted from jumping around pretending to play with her heroes. Dunks sat up.

DUNKS

Finally something different!

KEITH

Shut up.

SG

Go for it, Ashley.

Ashley searched and pulled up the Magic Dusters clip from CBGB.

SG

Ah. All of us have seen this.

I didn't want to burst her bubble. But like Dunks said, we wanted something new, and I had pretty much run that video into the ground.

Ashley held her hand out as if telling me to relax.

ASHLEY

This isn't what I want to show you, though. It's this one.

On the screen comes . . . us. All five of us. Soundtrack. The title says, "SOUNDTRACK PERFORMS SURPRISE SHOW AT 125TH," and under it, "This is my brother's band."

We all stared at the screen, watching us do our thing. Dunks on guitar. Keith on trumpet. Me on buckets. Alexis on bass. And Frankie on megaphone.

KEITH

Oh my God.

The shaky cell phone video wasn't the best quality, but it was good enough to see us rocking, to tell we were really in the flow, that moment where everything—every worry, every concern, every everything—goes away, and all that's left is the music.

The camera panned over and got a shot of the crowd, which looked way bigger on camera. The lady doing all the old dances, her arms whipping around. The sweat dripping down people's faces as they laughed and laughed. Everyone, including us, was alive. That was the only way I could really describe it. Alive.

DUNKS

This is us! This is us!

SG

It's crazy.

I paid close attention to it all. Watching Alexis lead the way with that soul-funk bass line. Until he didn't.

Until he dropped out. And the camera panned the crowd again, now catching the cops. Then the music stopped altogether. Then the lineup, the standoff. Looking at Keith stand there in front of Alexis, scared but strong. And Dunks, the same. No tears, no fear. And then to see myself step up there was like looking at someone else. Like it was me. So weird.

No one said a word. We all just watched ourselves. The rant from the crowd was loud, and you could hear people screaming things at the cops. A voice really close to the camera said, "Y'all could use a little music yourselves!"

SG

That was *you*?

ASHLEY

Yeah.

Her face was somewhere between happy, sad, and embarrassed.

And as Alexis stepped through the wall we built for him, and the cops put the cuffs on him, the video ended.

Keith let out a big sigh as the stress of it all climbed back on top of us. Back into us. Dunks leaned forward and tucked his head between his knees. I looked at Ashley, who sat on the floor, her face so innocent, now super worried.

ASHLEY

I'm sorry. I just thought you guys would get a kick out of that first part. I didn't—

SG

It's okay. It was really cool. We've never seen ourselves play before. Thank you.

Keith looked over at her and dug deep to shake it all off to say:

KEITH

Yeah, it really was cool.

Her mouth turned up just enough to not be a frown.

DUNKS

Plus ain't no point in stressing.

Dunks's voice was muffled, but he lifted his head.

DUNKS

Alexis should be out tomorrow, if Stuy's plan works.

KEITH

What plan? I don't know about no plan.

SG

Because it's mine and not yours. Don't worry about it.

I gave her a little attitude back, showing off for my sister. I couldn't help it.

Ashley smiled. Keith just looked at me blank.

KEITH

Okay, Stuy. I'm gonna let you have this one. But I hope it works.

SG

It will.

At least I hoped it would. It *had* to, or we were screwed.

KEITH

Anyway, Ashley, tell us about yourself.

SG

She's fifteen.

KEITH

What does that mean?

SG

It means she's a kid.

ASHLEY

I'm sixteen.

KEITH

She's sixteen. Which just means you're not cooler than a sixteen-year-old.

DUNKS

Ohhhhhh.

SG

Man, shut up! You're just upset about having a bird chest!

Ashley thought all of this was hilarious. Then she went into her story about our father, and the music, and about how she plays but is now doing more stuff on the production side. All that.

Dunks and Keith seemed to like her a lot, which was good because I really wanted them to. I mean, she's the only sibling I have. And even though we were just getting to know each other, I wanted to keep her around.

The funny thing was that Ashley had to tell the whole story twice, because right at the end of it all, when she talked about her father—our father—passing away from a heart attack, which I didn't know, there was a knock at Dunks's door.

Dunks went to see who it was.

DUNKS

Lucky?

My uncle Lucky came almost tiptoeing in, stepping over the coffee cups, the dingy T-shirts, the milk crates, and the wires. Behind him was a lady.

UNCLE LUCKY

```
Soundtrack!
```

He was bobbing his head as if there was music playing. Then he reached out for Keith's hand.

UNCLE LUCKY

I don't think we've met. Lucky.

KEITH

I'm Keith.

SG

Uncle Lucky. How'd you know I was here?

UNCLE LUCKY

Because you're always here, nephew. You remember Lisa, right?

SG

It was just yesterday.

I waved to her.

LISA

Hi, baby.

She was sort of posted up by the door, where it was safe for a lady in high heels. Then Uncle Lucky turned to Ashley.

UNCLE LUCKY

Is this . . .

SG

Uncle Lucky, this is Ashley, my sister. Ashley, Uncle Lucky.

Ashley stood up to shake his hand, but Uncle Lucky pulled her in for a hug. It was all so extra, but I appreciated it. Of course it would've been too easy to come in, meet her, and leave. Of course my uncle wanted the whole rundown. Who are you? Who's your mama? Where's that daddy of yours? And on and on. So Ashley repeated the story.

Once Lucky and Lisa left—yes, Lisa stood by the door the whole time, looking absolutely terrified to come any farther—me, Dunks, Keith, and Ashley spent the rest of the day acting stupid. We all took turns playing air instruments—me on the air drums, Dunks on the air guitar, and Keith again on the air horn.

Ashley showed us her best air bass guitar, which was pretty damn good. We could definitely tell she really played. She had a great stance, and her bass face was nasty. Almost as good as Alexis's. Dunks ordered a ton of Spanish food from around the corner, and we chowed down on chicken and yellow rice, plantains, and lime soda until we were stuffed and left loafing around Dunks's pigsty, which also happened to be an artist's heaven.

ASHLEY

I gotta boogie in a minute. Take that long ride home.

I sat next to her on the floor. We put our legs together and balanced the Styrofoam food container on top. There was nothing left in it but greasy yellow streaks and bone.

SG

I'm glad you came to hang with us. Next time, we'll actually do something.

ASHLEY

Please, this was cool.

KEITH

Yeah, feel free to come kick it whenever. You're so much cooler than your big brother.

She threw a piece of gristle at me.

SG

Whatever.

ASHLEY

I don't know. He's pretty cool.

Little sisters aren't so bad. Perfect for ego boosts.

Dunks was nodding off on the couch. After what he told me about his mother, and having to go see her early in the morning, every morning, it explained why he looked like he never slept. Because he never did.

Keith slapped him on the leg.

DUNKS

What?

SG

Ashley is about to bounce.

DUNKS

Oh. So good meeting you.

Dunks rocked himself back and forth on the couch trying to get enough momentum to stand.

DUNKS

You gotta come back so you can meet Alexis and Frankie.

Ashley stood as well, and Keith and I followed suit.

ASHLEY

I will.

Hugs all around. Two for me, the second one being longer and tighter. It felt good knowing we had the same blood. That we were brother and sister. That was new for me, but she came at the perfect time.

ASHLEY

And I know you guys are a band, and I totally respect that, but if for some reason you need a stand-in on bass until everything works out with Alexis, let me know. I'm nowhere near as good as he is, but I can hold on my own.

SG

Plus, you're family.

I knew we would never play without Alexis. But it felt good saying that, and I really did appreciate the offer.

ASHLEY

Exactly.

She grabbed her purse and dusted off her butt.

ASHLEY

Also, if you guys ever need some free studio time, it's far, but it's open to you. I'm much better at that kind of stuff than at playing the bass.

SG

That I might have to take you up on.

ASHLEY

Like you said . . .

She looked over my shoulder at the other two.

ASHLEY

. . . we're family.

CHAPTER 18

MONDAY. ALEXIS'S LOCKUP DAY NUMBER THREE. MOST OF the day was spent sitting on the steps in Union Square, trying to decide whether or not we should go to Harlem to see if we could pay his bail. But what Keith and Dunks and Frankie didn't know was that we didn't have the money to do that anymore. So while they were trying to decide if we were heading uptown, I was praying we wouldn't, and sneak-texting my mother.

is he gonna drop the charges???

I hoped my mother knew the rule about the three question marks.

i dont know

How could she not know? I mean, come on!

did you try to convince him?

Buzz.

of course.

Another buzz.

but i dont know

Meanwhile, Keith was pacing back and forth, up and down the steps, trying to come up with a game plan.

KEITH

I don't wanna go all the way up there and they tell us we can't see him again.

SG

Or that his bail is set dumb high, like twenty grand.

KEITH

Why would it be that high, Stuy? All he did was punch somebody.

SG

Yeah, to us. But Dummy said he was assaulted. I feel like that word adds on a few thousand dollars.

KEITH

True. What you think, Frankie?

Frankie sat on a step sipping water. He looked exhausted, especially for a kid so young. I figured he was just as stressed out as the rest of us. Plus he was coming off a weekend of being sick.

FRANKIE

I think we wait. I mean, Stuy said he had a plan, so let's just see what happens.

SG

Exactly.

I was relieved that the thirteen-year-old had some sense.

Dunks didn't say much of anything. He just lay flat on his back on the top step with his eyes closed. The sun beamed on his pale face, and an occasional shadow of a pigeon would darken parts of it every few minutes.

KEITH

So what now?

Keith finally took a seat. I checked my phone to see if my mother had said anything else. She hadn't.

SG

Now we figure out what we're gonna do when he's out. Like, where we're gonna play and all that, because every day we're not playing, people are losing interest in us.

KEITH

You seen those YouTube hits?

FRANKIE

We're on YouTube?

KEITH

Yeah, I'll show you later. Like twenty or thirty thousand people had seen it in two days. And those comments!

SG

I know. Insane! That's why we gotta do something soon. While we're hot!

Dunks opened his eyes. He slowly sat up.

DUNKS

I think we go big.

He was so sure, so confident, that we all were waiting to see what he had.

DUNKS

I say we take it to Times Square.

Then he lay back down and closed his eyes like some kind of monk.

We all sat there for a second, letting Dunks's statement sink in. But we never said anything, because we already knew that he was right.

But what I wasn't so sure of was whether or not Alexis was actually going to get out. Time seemed to move slower and slower, everybody checking their phones to see if he had texted or called. Nothing. Hour after hour. Nothing. I texted my mother a few more times. Nothing.

Union Square was buzzing with people as usual. Hippies and stay-at-homers hitting up the farmers market, skaters and all the resident weird kids, which I guess we were now sort of a part of, the nannies pushing strollers of other people's kids, the old men playing chess, the monks who chant and ring that bell, dancing in a line.

Everybody was out there, yet for us, no one was out there. It was like the four of us sat on those steps alone, all day long, waiting for our fifth. And he didn't come. Or call.

Seven o'clock. The farmers market was gone, leaving bits of hay and random veggie leaves behind. The nannies gone, now home probably taking care of their own kids. The monks gone, the peaceful chanting gone with them, giving way to the loud cussing of the weird kids who were still there. Like us. Still there.

Keith finally stood up.

KEITH

Yo, this is for the birds. I don't know what your plan is, but I think it's time to go get our boy.

SG

But we don't even know how much his bail is going to be. It could be crazy.

I stood up, hoping they would buy in just a little longer.

KEITH

Or it might not be. We got, what, about three grand saved up? What if that's enough?

SG

How you know his parents ain't gonna bail him out?

KEITH

Because they already told me they didn't have it. I went over there, remember?

Keith's arms moved like she was doing different kinds of karate moves.

KEITH

I wrote on a piece of paper what happened. Mr. and Mrs. Brown read it and cried like babies. That's why I'm not waiting around no more.

FRANKIE

Yeah, we gotta do something.

KEITH

We owe it to him, Stuy. Come on, man.

Dunks stood up to stretch.

DUNKS

She's right, man. Your plan ain't work. It's time for plan B.

KEITH

Exactly. Which is to go to your crib, get our money, and then shoot up to Harlem and get our boy out. That's it.

SG

That's *not* it. It's not that simple.

My voice and heart fluttered at the same time.

Dunks and Frankie looked confused, but Keith just looked wound up. Like she was literally ready to go break this man out of jail. Like she could put her fists through the brick or bend the bars.

KEITH

It *is*, Stuy. You the only one overthinking it, when really, at this point, you should be doing whatever it takes to get Alexis home!

Keith had that look in her eyes again.

I sat back down on the steps.

SG

That's the thing, though. I did do whatever it took. Look, there's no point trying to bail him out.

KEITH

What?!

Keith cocked her head to the side like I was speaking another language. Then, I just said it.

SG

There's no money.

Everybody's eyes got wide. It almost felt like every single person in Union Square was looking straight at me. My stomach began to turn, and my heart banged in my chest hard enough to explode. I could feel myself coming apart right there on those steps, but what was even more scary was knowing it wasn't going to just be me that was shattered. It was going to be everything. All of us. This friendship, this family. Over.

SG

```
I used it.
```

I had to stop because my tongue was dry, and it felt like I was trying to talk with dirt in my mouth. I tried to create spit, but none would come.

SG

```
I used it to pay my mother's boyfriend
off, hoping that he'd drop the charges.
```

DUNKS

You did *what*?

KEITH

```
Wait. Wait, wait, wait. You've gotta be
kidding me. This has to be a joke. Tell
me you're joking, Stuy. Tell me this is a
joke. Tell me this is a joke, Stuy!
```

Frankie just sat there quiet, but I could tell he was mad too.

SG

```
I wish it was.
```

My phone buzzed, but this wasn't a good time to check it. Not with such a shitstorm brewing.

KEITH

```
So if this dude decides to keep the
money, we're just assed out?
```

I didn't say anything. I just looked up at her. And when our eyes met, she charged me.

SG

```
I was trying to do the right thing!
```

DUNKS

```
The right thing? The right thing?
```

Dunks held her while she swung her arms at me.

I knew that people were watching, but it didn't really matter. I couldn't really worry about all that with Keith yelling and screaming at me.

KEITH

I can't *believe* you! I can't believe you could be so stupid! Stupid, stupid, stupid!

Dunks struggled to pull her back. I could feel myself getting emotional, but crying was not an option. I had to hold it in. To make a point.

I tried to do what was right, and even though I was sorry it wasn't going like I thought it would, at least I tried to make it right. That's what I told her.

KEITH

```
You picked the wrong time to not be a
pussy, Stuy.
```

That one cut me deep. So deep that I couldn't really say anything back. I just nodded and decided that my time in Union Square was over for the night. I walked off.

Whispers surrounded me like ghosts. My phone buzzed again. I checked it.

2 MISSED CALLS FROM ALEXIS

I whipped around back toward the steps. Frankie answered his phone and put one hand in the air.

Thumbs up.

AN HOUR LATER, THE MOMENT we were waiting for. It felt like we were anticipating Michael Jackson. It was that big, that important. And there he was. The giant came stomping up the steps from the subway station.

KEITH

Man, what took so long?

ALEXIS

My phone was dead. Had to charge it before I could call y'all. Got out a few hours ago.

Alexis had the brightest smile in the world on his face. He gave Dunks the secret handshake, then Frankie. He hugged Keith, lifting her off the ground, squeezing her until she chopped at his shoulders. Then I stepped up.

Me and Alexis did the secret handshake, but at the end of it he pulled me in for a hug.

SG

Thank you.

ALEXIS

Man, thank *you*!

He pushed me away.

ALEXIS

I would've killed you if you ain't get me out of there, knowhatimsayin'?

KEITH

That woulda made two of us!

We kicked it in our favorite pizza shop the rest of the night, catching Alexis up on Ashley and how awesome she was. We told him that we were thinking about maybe using her recording studio in the Bronx to cut a record. Maybe. I mean, it was a good option since we had no money, but we explained to Alexis that we were still going to try to make the cash back by taking over Times Square, so we could possibly still record in a big-time studio, like Electric Lady, where Hendrix did his thing.

Besides that, we all just listened to Alexis's ridiculous jail stories, which were really more for Dunks and Frankie than for me and Keith. He went on and on about some dude named Kung Fu Joe who was locked up with him.

ALEXIS

Man, Joe was like this weird-ass black dude who did everything fast. He talked fast, he walked fast, he ate fast. And he wore one of them kung fu outfits. Dude was wild.

DUNKS

What was he in there for?

Dunks slurped up a dangling piece of cheese.

ALEXIS

For nunchucking a dude on the bus!

SG

What?

ALEXIS

Yo, I'm dead serious. That's what he told me. Joe said some young dude was talking smack to this girl, straight-up disrespecting her, knowhatimsayin'? So . . .

Alexis flung his arms around like he had nunchucks.

ALEXIS

. . . BAM! 'Chucked him up!

And as if the longest weekend ever didn't just happen, things were pretty much back to normal.

For the next three days, Soundtrack was operating like a machine. We knew that Times Square had to happen soon, so we chose Friday. We also knew that we had been off the grid for a few, and that we would need to figure out how to let people know that we were going to be there.

I mean, of course it was Times Square, and there were always people—too many people—there.

But most of them were tourists. And tourists were cool, but they were here today and back to their hometowns tomorrow. We needed our regulars. Our people.

So we came up with a few ideas. Number one: We reached out to Dylan, our faithful promoter. We told her that Alexis was home and that we were planning a big move—taking our show to the biggest station in the city. All we needed her to do was talk about it. Tweet it. Post about it on Facebook. I mean, information can reach to the other side of the world in three seconds, so with three days, we figured we should be okay with Dylan just doing these small things.

Number two: I called Ashley and asked her to make a YouTube video. I explained that all we wanted it to say was SOUNDTRACK. THIS FRIDAY. TIMES SQUARE NYC. That's all. Keep it mysterious.

And number three: Tell Dylan about this YouTube video, just in case she wanted to use it for an extra boost.

Other than that, the five of us together again practiced our asses off, day in, day out.

Not any one particular song, because that wasn't really our thing. We just wanted to give Alexis time to get his groove back after all the crap that went on, which didn't take him long at all. I mean, he really fell right back in like he never left, and he was so excited to play—so happy just to touch his bass and look around the room at all of us—that he was rocking on another level.

Matter fact, most of the jam sessions were really just us standing around listening to Alexis cut loose. Just shocked at how good he was. He was only gone for, really, just two days, but it was like we were hearing him for the first time.

DUNKS

```
Yo, if this is what jail does to a
musician, send me!
```

Dunks gripped his pink guitar. Such a stupid thing to say, but secretly that's how we all felt.

Dunks had pretty much let me abandon all my super duties for the week, and because of that, by Thursday Ms. Dyson had come downstairs and taped her concerns to his door. She needed to know how to open the windows, and once they were opened, how to close them. And also if she could have the autographs of the rest of the members of the band.

Mr. Garcia just came and knocked on the door to let us know that he finally finished a chapter.

DUNKS

```
No paper in the toilet, Mr. Garcia.
```

MR. GARCIA

```
No, sir. None to throw in there, Duncan.
I'm keeping it all!
```

Mr. Garcia threw that gummy smile at us, waving a stack of paper.

The Bednicks had been doing okay for a while. No crazy girlfriends. No broken windows. We just hoped it stayed that way, at least until after Friday.

And last but not least, on Thursday, as we were playing around, someone knocked at the door. Dunks opened it. He stood there for a while talking to the person, until finally he invited them in.

DUNKS

```
Guys . . .
```

He moved his guitar so it hung behind him.

DUNKS

```
This is my mom.
```

KEITH

```
Hey.
```

FRANKIE

```
Nice to meet you.
```

We all gave her hugs, which she clearly wasn't ready for. She almost curled into a ball when Alexis opened his arms to her. She was young, younger than I imagined, but she moved like she was old. She was dressed in flannel pajamas, and her hair was stuffed under a black baseball cap with MISFITS on it. Clearly Dunks's hat. She took a seat in the corner and watched us practice. And that night, no joke, Dunks played like an alien.

CHAPTER 19

FRIDAY. GAME TIME. SHOWTIME. WHATEVER YOU WANNA call it, it was time. Everybody met at Dunks's like usual. We had our ritual before-show meal, arroz con pollo, talking trash and teasing each other while Alexis pounded back lime soda to see how loud and long he could belch. Good to have him back.

Frankie stood in front of this old mirror that Dunks kept against the wall to watch himself practice. He rehearsed the line over and over again:

FRANKIE

Yes, I'm Famous Frankie. How do you do?

We all joked him about it.

ALEXIS

I mean, really, Frankie? How do you do?
Boy, you from Brooklyn!

FRANKIE

Y'all wouldn't understand.

Then he continued practicing how to be a star. Keith jumped around like she was a boxer, making weird spit sounds, trying to get the nerves out. Dunks just closed his eyes like he was meditating, holding his hands in the air and wiggling his fingers. I heard Alexis call that spirit fingers. And I went over different drum patterns, slapping the sticks against my thighs over and over again until I was sure they left welts.

Before we knew it, we were out the door and on the train. And all I kept thinking was what if all these people were going to the same place we were going? What if they were all riding this train to Times Square to see us? I even thought I heard someone say something about going to see a band, but I wasn't sure.

I was just so anxious. I could tell that all of us were. None of us said a word the whole way. Just lost in our own thoughts, I guess. Dunks, Keith, Alexis, and Frankie were probably all thinking the same things I was thinking. That this is all so amazing. That this is the best feeling in the world.

Once we got off the train, we figured we'd set up right in the tunnel where the A train comes, just because that's also where all the people have to come through to get to the Port Authority Bus Terminal.

Times Square is different from every other station in New York, mainly because of the amount of people who get on and get off there. We found a spot to set up everything. Right in front of one of those snack vendors, a little ways down from the bus gate.

ALEXIS

```
Aight. Let's get together quick. I'm
ready to do this.
```

Him and Dunks got their instruments all rigged up with the car battery and everything, while Keith used her shirt to polish her horn.

DYLAN

Hey, guys.

EVERYBODY

Dylan!
Dylan!
Dylannnnn!

SG

Yo, yo! Good to see you.

DYLAN

Good to see you too! Especially you.

ALEXIS

Yeah, you know, I was jammed up for a second, but I'm good to go.

He slowly pulled the guitar from the black case, like lifting a body from a grave.

DYLAN

I'm so excited. I did everything. Text messages, emails, Facebook, everything.

I sat on my crate and moved the buckets around to make sure they were in the right place.

SG

We definitely appreciate it. So what's it gonna be tonight? You hanging back here with us, or you partying in the crowd?

DYLAN

Oh, I'm partying!

Dylan threw her hands up and did some weird white-girl shake. Keith just busted out laughing and mouthed to me, *I love her.*

Dunks plucked his strings and twisted the tuning knobs. Twisting, plucking. Twisting, plucking. Alexis did the same thing. Keith was now blowing and spitting, playing a few random low notes that sounded like farts echoing through the tunnel.

People started to gather slowly. Some—a lot—had roller bags. They were the newbies. And some I actually recognized from Harlem. A few I even recognized from all the way back at West Fourth. The diehard fans who really loved to see us rock. The old heads and the young folks. The freaks, the geeks, and the sneaks. The suits and the slobs. The skaters, the daters, and the haters who just couldn't seem to hate us.

We waited, watching the crowd grow, some people calling out to us, "No cops this time!" and everybody clapping and laughing, waiting for the jam. It was like Alexis's arrest made us even more popular.

Like we were rappers or something.

I saw one girl hold a sign up that said THE SOUNDTRACK OF THE CITY, and as she pushed through the crowd, I realized it was Ashley. Hell yeah.

Cell phones were already out, people taking pictures and videotaping us, and we weren't even playing yet. Magazine people asking if they could interview us after we were done. Crazy. Perfect families, moms and dads with their young kids sitting up on their shoulders. My old band teacher Mr. Rochester showed up. Uncle Lucky with Lisa. Frankie's mom came, of course, running over to kiss him. Frankie wasn't too happy about that. I mean, this was Famous Frankie, not no mama's boy. Alexis's parents came, standing with their shoes off, hoping they could tell the difference between his rumble and the trains. Keith's dad came—Keith Sr.—and he stood in the front, nudging my uncle, pointing to Keith proudly. I had never seen him before. He had freckles just like she did. But he wasn't nearly as pretty.

DUNKS

`Let's just wait it out.`

Dunks stood there with his guitar strapped across his chest, PLUTO on the front for everyone to see. We all just stood there looking at everyone, watching as the crowd came pouring down the corridor, growing and growing. It was bigger than any of us could've imagined. And it only took one person to set it off.

That person was Uncle Lucky, who, like he said, still had some crazy left in him. Uncle Lucky started chanting low.

UNCLE LUCKY

`Soundtrack. Soundtrack. Soundtrack.`

Keith's father joined in, and so did Lisa and Ashley and Dylan.

CROWD

`Soundtrack! Soundtrack! Soundtrack!`

It started spreading, each person joining in as it got bigger and bigger, louder and louder, until the chant of "Soundtrack!" was louder than the screaming trains whooshing all around us.

We all looked at each other. No. Way. We couldn't believe what was happening. This was our moment.

Frankie put Keith's trumpet case between us and the mob, then put his megaphone to his mouth and started chanting with the people. He just couldn't control himself, and I couldn't blame him. It was time.

FRANKIE

```
Everybody gather round! Come grab hold
of a brand-new sound!
```

Frankie threw his head back and yelled through the megaphone:

FRANKIE

```
Say it with me, y'all!
```

ALMOST EVERYONE

```
We! Are! Soundtrack!
```

Dunks looked over at me and nodded. That meant it was on me. I sat on the crate, pulled my sticks out, and didn't know what to play. It was like I blanked out. I don't know if all the hype got to me or what. But I froze up.

Alexis turned to make sure I was okay. He just nodded, which was his way of saying "Go ahead."

Then Keith nodded, and from her it was:

KEITH

```
What the hell are you doing?
```

SG

```
Frankie, follow me.
```

Frankie nodded, which meant:

FRANKIE

```
Hell yeah.
```

All this in about ten seconds, which felt like ten minutes. I started smacking the drumsticks together. Clack, clack, clack, clack. Frankie knew exactly what to do.

FRANKIE

Everybody, tonight we need y'all help! Can you help us out?

CROWD

Yeah!

FRANKIE

Alright, so let me see you put your hands together to the beat!

Frankie pulled the megaphone away from his mouth to demonstrate. The crowd was right with him, clapping, clapping, clapping, clapping.

Clack, clack, clack, clack. I kept up the beat, then out of nowhere, I threw a stomp in there. Clack, clack, clack-stomp, clack. Clack, clack, clack-stomp, clack.

FRANKIE

Now just this side over here. Y'all gonna throw that stomp in there. Got me?

Everybody was with him, and the whole left side of the crowd was right on time with the stomp. Well, not everybody. There were a few random offbeats. But for the most part, the stomps were on point.

Then I added one more trick in there. A double stomp. Clack-stomp-stomp, clack, clack-stomp, clack. Clack-stomp-stomp, clack, clack-stomp, clack.

FRANKIE

Now this is for all y'all over here right side. Y'all can do this! Just those two stomps in the beginning. The left side's got the last one.

Frankie was strutting around cheering on what had become literally a crowd full of cheerleaders. It was ridiculous, but everyone was doing it.

FRANKIE

Y'all ready?

The right side howled. And got to it. Clack-stomp-stomp, clack, clack-stomp, clack. They were spot on. And we were ready to party.

FRANKIE

See, this is about all of us! We're all Soundtrack!

He looked back at the band, everyone grinning and nodding like weirdos.

FRANKIE

Keep that beat going!

And like the most perfect thing you ever heard, in came the bass. Alexis popped the strings so hard that you could feel the vibration, like squirrels running around in the pit of your stomach. His parents opened up their mouths wide and held up the "I love you" sign. Thumb out, pointer and pinkie up, middle and ring down.

He played a few bars before Keith came jabbing in with the

horn over top of that. It was bluesy, almost churchy, and meshed with the bass. Times Square was getting ready to become one of those old-school juke joints you see in old movies, where women get flipped up in the air and all that.

The crowd went wild when the sound of the trumpet sat on top of that bass line and rode it like the A to Brooklyn. Or Harlem. And when Dunks decided to jump on in the water with us, the crowd went nuts.

Dunks took it easy, though, only hitting notes on the claps, but leaving the stomps empty. Each clap became lightning when Dunks struck a note. He rocked his body back and forth like a man possessed. I could hear my uncle wooooooooooing from the front line, watching Dunks give that alien-funk, that Pluto Music to the people.

We held it steady, right there for a while, letting it seep in. It was a heavy groove, raw and rugged, yet undeniable. I stood up on my crate, still clacking the sticks together. All those people—strangers, fans, friends, family—all were moving at the same time, feeling the same things, doing the same things. It was like a routine, as if we had rehearsed this whole thing, but we hadn't. The music was doing it. The music was doing it!

Finally, after about ten minutes of that, I actually started playing the beat on the buckets, to break the people out of their trance and really get the party started. And boy oh boy, did the party get started!

We cut loose, and the crowd went wild, dancing and shouting and clapping. The teenagers partied with the old people, and the freaks partied with the suits. And after a good while of sweaty fun, Frankie decided to dance all through the crowd, and I just knew that at some point as he tunneled into the sea of people, he would soon be lifted up and there would be some kind of rock star crowd-surfing thing that could only happen to the one and only Famous Frankie.

But Frankie was never lifted. And he never came out of the crowd.

There was a sound. A strange sound. The squealing feedback from the megaphone, coupled with horrible screams.

Everyone shuffled around, bumping into each other, some trying to get out, some trying to get in, until finally someone yelled, "Call 911!"

Not again.

We threw our instruments down and rushed through the crowd, squeezing past people, Alexis physically moving folks out of the way.

Everyone became nothing more than a blur of colors, their voices muted as if we were all underwater. By the time we got to him, his mother was right with us, worry pouring from her like sweat.

FRANKIE'S MOM

Frankie!

ALEXIS

Give her space! Back up! Back up!

The man holding Frankie was calm. But Frankie wasn't. His body jumped and shook, as if he was being electrocuted. His eyes were rolled back in his head, and the man cradled him on his side while Frankie kicked around like a fish out of water.

His mother dropped to her knees and whispered to him, her hand gently wiping his forehead.

FRANKIE'S MOM

It's okay, baby. It's okay. Come on, Frankie. Come out of it. Come out of it.

Then she looked up at us, the four of us, Dunks, Keith, Alexis, and me, and yelled:

FRANKIE'S MOM

Someone call 911!

She repeated it, and that time it was like I had just come up from underwater and could hear. Like someone just unpaused life and suddenly everything was real again. Real.

I pulled my phone out. No service underground.

I broke out and sprinted down the corridor toward the exit, other people doing the same. Yelling at the MTA lady behind the glass. Looking for alarms to pull like the ones they have on the trains.

Madness.

When I got to the stairwell that led outside, I looked at my phone and dialed the three digits: 911. My hands were sopping wet, but I was still able to get it done. Just like Lucky taught me.

It rang once. Then a lady picked up, her voice calm.

STUY'S MOM

911 Emergency.

Silence for a second. I couldn't speak, struck by everything. Frankie, and now this. Then, again:

STUY'S MOM

911 Emergency. Hello?

SG

Mom?

STUY'S MOM

Stuy?

CHAPTER 20

IF THERE WAS A MOVIE MADE ABOUT MY LIFE, IT WOULD start with me, Uncle Lucky, and his friend Spit in the kitchen of our apartment. I'd be six, and I'd have on my favorite red socks. The ones my big toes stuck out. Uncle Lucky would be explaining to me for the hundredth time:

UNCLE LUCKY

Nephew, anything happens, you call 911.

Then he'd put one bullet in his pistol and spin the cylinder. Spit would take a long pull on a joint and let the stinky smoke float to the ceiling, while Uncle Lucky cocked the gun and lifted it to his head. Then, Uncle Lucky, with his finger on the trigger, would close his eyes and say:

UNCLE LUCKY

Lucky, lucky, lucky.

And BAM! The title of the movie in big bold letters would pop up on the screen: THE STORY OF STUYVESANT GREY.

ALEXIS

Uhhh.

Alexis sorta groaned, looking around at Keith, Frankie, and Dunks.

ALEXIS

Dude. That's pretty intense, knowhatimsayin'?

Alexis stuffed his hand into the bag of chips we were sharing and pulled out a fistful. He passed the bag to Frankie.

KEITH

Right! I mean, damn, Stuy. You couldn't have just started your movie with you sitting at the buckets doing a count-off or something?

SG

I mean, that's how I would start my movie. *My* movie. What y'all would do is on y'all. But me, that's how my flick begins. What about you, Dunks? Alexis already said his would start with him stringing his bass and turning the amp all the way up. Keith told us how hers would basically be her in the bathroom mirror shaving her head.

KEITH

I said that would be part of it. Then after the hair was gone, I would pick up my horn. And then you'd get this dope shot of me—

ALEXIS

Yeah, yeah, we got it.

Keith screwed her face up and threw a fake punch.

ALEXIS

Dunks, what about you?

DUNKS

Aight, check it. It starts off in space—

FRANKIE

Come on, man.

ALEXIS

Dunks, dude, you're not an alien! Get over it. You're from the Lower East Side!

SG

Let it go, man. Just let it go.

DUNKS

I play like an alien, though. Right or wrong?

Nobody said nothing. We all just looked away like somebody invisible was calling out our names.

DUNKS

Haters!

He snatched the bag of chips from Frankie, who was just holding the bag but not eating any.

KEITH

Okay, okay, okay, what about you, Frankie? How would your movie start?

Frankie sat there for a second, looking around at all of us.

FRANKIE

Well, I guess it would start the day I met y'all. My crew. The band.

KEITH

You met me first, so technically the story starts with me. But I'll let it slide just so we don't make these fools jealous.

ALEXIS

Oh, please!

DUNKS

I used to give you money for pizza!

FRANKIE

I mean, what does it matter for anyway? We ain't making no movies. I mean, we make music. Matter fact, we make magic.

KEITH

Got that right.

Her eyes watered as she looked at the newspaper clip of us beside Frankie's hospital bed. What the doctors told his mother, and what she told us, was that Frankie's cancer had come back and had already spread to his brain, which caused him to have that seizure in the subway station.

No one saw it coming. Not the doctors, not anyone. And once we knew what was happening, there really wasn't much anyone could do. It was like all of a sudden this kid went from healthy, to having a few weird headaches, to lying in a bed with his friends gathered around, fading away.

ALEXIS

Speaking of music, give me a beat, Stuy.

I patted a beat on my chest and thighs, while Alexis made a bass line with his mouth. Dunks didn't make a sound until he heard Keith begin to sing to Frankie in that weird, froggy Louis Armstrong voice. Then we all funked it up a little, y'know, to make it our own:

KEITH

I see trees of green, red roses too
I see 'em bloom, for me and for you
And I think to myself,
What a wonderful world.

FAMOUS FRANKIE PASSED AWAY a week after that. We had been to the hospital every single day up until then, laughing, taking pictures, videotaping, and just being a band—a family. We had Frankie sign autographs for us and promised him that if we sold them, it would be for no less than a million dollars. That made him smile.

We used the money that we earned from the Times Square show to help Frankie's mother pay for the funeral. It was the right thing to do, and like I said, we had a pretty good plan B in Ashley.

The funeral was at a small church in Bay Ridge. I had never been to Bay Ridge before. Frankie's mother asked us to carry the casket out of the church after the funeral, which I had also never done. But of course I said yes. We all did.

She also asked if we could play a song at the service. Again, we couldn't say no, even though none of us had ever played a funeral before. But Frankie was one of us, so it had to be done.

After all the prayers, and the sermon, the youth choir singing, and everybody crying, Frankie's mother came up to the podium. She was a small round woman with a face like sunshine, even on such a sad day.

FRANKIE'S MOM

My son Frankie spent the last summer of his life around music. Some of you may not have known that he had joined a band with his dear friend and guardian angel, Keith.

Frankie's mother looked over at us—at Keith—who began to shake and frantically wipe tears from her cheeks as if she was trying to rub her freckles off.

FRANKIE'S MOM

And through Keith, Frankie met Alexis, Stuyvesant, and Duncan—

Dunks squirmed in his seat at the sound of his government name.

FRANKIE'S MOM

Or Dunks, as they call him.

She smiled.

FRANKIE'S MOM

It was with this bunch that he was given a chance to really find himself and be himself. He would come home—whenever Keith got him there on time—and he'd be going on and on about Dunks and his Pluto Music . . .

Dunks's eyes got wide, and his teeth nearly jumped out of his mouth.

FRANKIE'S MOM

And how Alexis can speak sign language. And Stuy's obsession with Savion Glover. And how Keith is the boss of them all.

Keith puffed up her chest, and the crowd laughed.

FRANKIE'S MOM

Please, you know good and well them boys take care of you.

She winked at Keith.

FRANKIE'S MOM

The point I'm making is Frankie—Famous

Frankie, as y'all called him—loved y'all. He was so grateful to be around you every day. To be a part of something so special.

Frankie's mom began to crumble. She fanned her face and did her best to pull it together.

FRANKIE'S MOM

And I just thank you so much for that.

She took a deep breath. Then she straightened up and addressed the crowd face-forward. She cleared her throat.

FRANKIE'S MOM

Now, in honor of my boy—I would do it like him, but I can't without crying—can you come play something for us?

We all nodded and began to stand.

FRANKIE'S MOM

Soundtrack, ladies and gentlemen!

She stepped down from the pulpit. The four of us walked to the front of the church, the crowd clapping hard. We stood in front of Frankie's casket, a bouquet of flowers lying across the top. I looked for familiar faces in the crowd. I spotted Dylan, who stood along the back wall. So nice of her to come. And not far from her, sitting on the edge of the back pew, was my mother.

We had been texting back and forth since the 911 call, mainly about how Frankie was doing. When she found out he had passed, she asked when and where the funeral was going to be. I told her, but I wasn't expecting her to come. But she did.

Keith ran her hand over the smooth wood of the casket before turning around and facing the people. Then she put her shiny horn up to her lips and blew air through, no spit.

Dunks's and Alexis's guitars were already plugged into the house speakers. They hoisted their instruments over their shoulders, Alexis's bass resting up on his belly as usual, and Dunks's pink Stratocaster hung low by his waist. They both turned the tuning knobs and plucked their strings softly, making sure the sound was right.

Even though the church had a real drum set, I brought my buckets anyway. I sat on the crate, pulled my drumsticks from my back pocket, and looked down the line to see the rest of the band.

Dunks, Keith, and Alexis all looked back at me, their faces somehow both sad and extremely proud. And at that moment I think we were all hoping that Frankie was right about what he said about the music. What all of us secretly believed.

That it was magic.

Soundtrack
PLAYLIST

Michael Jackson: "Off the Wall"

Sly and the Family Stone: "Everybody Is a Star"

The Temptations: "Papa Was a Rollin' Stone"

Bob Marley: "Trenchtown Rock"

Nas: "N.Y. State of Mind"

Jimi Hendrix: "Freedom"

Stevie Wonder: "Contusion"

Herbie Hancock: "Watermelon Man"

Diana Ross and the Supremes: "Reflections"

Jackson 5: "The Love You Save"

Marvin Gaye: "Trouble Man"

Louis Armstrong: "What a Wonderful World"

The Beatles: "Blackbird"

AUTHOR Q&A

1. What was your inspiration for writing *Soundtrack*?

I wanted to explore what it means to be a young artist searching for community and family among other artists. This is a book for the artists.

2. Why was *Soundtrack* published as an audiobook first?

You know, I wrote this book a long time ago, but for whatever reason, it was in the drawer, which is basically my personal slush pile. When PRH/Listening Library came asking for original works, Elena (my agent) brought it up, and I'm glad she did because it worked perfectly for what they were looking for. It's a book about music, so it almost makes more sense to hear it first.

3. Obvious, but we couldn't resist: Do you play any instruments? If not, what instrument would you *want* to play?

I've fooled around on the guitar for years, but I've also tried a lot of instruments. Gave the trumpet a go when I was young. I've tried the harmonica. I've messed around with the bass guitar. Anything that makes a sound. I've even tried the kalimba.

4. What kind of music did you listen to when you were a teen? Did you have any favorite musicians or artists?

I listened to a little bit of everything. I was an eclectic kid, and my father had broad musical tastes. So I was influenced by a lot of what he listened to, which was Hall and Oates, Phil Collins, The Police, Ray Charles, Taj Mahal, James Brown, Peter Frampton, Buddy Guy, Bob Marley, the Talking Heads, Tears for Fears, Ace of Base, and on and on and on. But, of course, I also loved hip-hop. Biggie and OutKast and Wu-Tang, Camp Lo, Mos Def, Tribe, De La, Latifah, Fugees, and the list goes on.

5. What music are you listening to right now? How has your music taste changed?

My taste hasn't really changed much. I'm pretty much wide open. Right now I'm listening to Chance's *Star Line* and JID's *God Does Like Ugly*. A lot of Clipse and Griselda. I'm listening to Hayley Williams's *Ego Death at a Bachelorette Party*, which is awesome. I'm still listening to the same kind of weird mix of stuff. A little rock and roll, a little alternative, and some old-school. You know, I've been listening to a lot of Sade. A lot of the Isley Brothers, who I think are the greatest band of all time. Of course, there's Stevie Wonder—the best solo artist of all time. I was walking around the city recently, listening to "The Secret Life of Plants" and thinking I love whatever this is. Honestly, I'm into and open to anything that moves me in any given moment.

6. You lived in New York City for a while. What was living in New York like? Are any of your experiences reflected in the novel? Do your New York years coincide with the time frame of *Soundtrack*?

When I lived in New York, I was much older than they are in the story, but I wrote it while still living there. I lived in Bed-Stuy, so Stuy's name obviously comes from the neighborhood I lived in for all those years, and it's reflective of my time there. I mean, there's nothing like New York City busking. If you go underground and you see the kids playing music, you're talking about geniuses who are beneath the earth. There's something about that that's just really fascinating. Like what does it mean to be a sixteen-year-old genius musician playing underground, in this dank, stinky, heavily populated, rat-infested place, and you're bringing beauty to it? You're bringing sound and life and creating a soundtrack—no pun intended—to the people passing through and sometimes to the people who dwell there. People going to work, people who sleep down there, kids who are headed to school with other kids, elders. There's something about that that is really, really fascinating to me. Even when it was annoying, because people who live in New York know that sometimes it can be a little annoying when the drummers come on the train or the dancers come on the train or whatever, there is still something about it that feels like the heartbeat of the city in an interesting, beautiful way.

None of my experiences living in New York are explicitly in the novel, but my best friend's sister is deaf. And so growing up, I got to learn about how to communicate with the hearing-impaired and how listening can be vibratory. That was something I pulled from my childhood that I was able to put in the story, for sure. Everything else is me considering who these young people are. I'd be waiting for, or be on, the train, and these kids are jamming, and there's a part of me that's just thinking, "Who are they? What are their stories? They didn't just end up here. And what about these kids? Where do they come from? Where do they go when they're done playing music? What are they doing with the money they've earned when they leave? Do they split it over a pizza pie? What happens to them when they walk out of the subway station?" These are the things that kind of sparked the story.

7. The band eats a lot of pizza. What is your favorite pizza place in NYC?

This spot that used to be called Ray's—yes, one of the many Rays—but now it's called Prince Street Pizza. That was, and probably still is, my favorite. Now there's a line outside every time you go, but I used to work around the corner, and you never had to wait for your slice. Now they have like a rope up and everything, which is weird. But I still rock with it—it's delicious.

8. The characters of *Soundtrack* also love to eat takeout arroz con pollo and lime soda. Did you have a favorite takeout place in NYC?

Not really, but if I really had to pick, for me, nothing beats a bodega hero. The honey-roasted turkey on a hero, with oil and vinegar and lettuce and tomato, salt and pepper, provolone, warmed up. Like, that was like my jam. And a bag of chips.

9. Stuy's mom teaches him how to drum in two ways: striking red and blue tape Xs to mimic drumming, and watching tap dancers like Savion Glover to learn beats. How did you come up with these cool ideas for learning music?

That's a hard question. I think I just love tap dancing. I love the Nicholas Brothers, Gregory Hines, and Sammy Davis Jr. I grew up watching them with my father. And then, when Savion Glover came onto the scene, it was different because he looked more like me and the people from my generation. He wasn't wearing a suit or trousers—he was wearing baggy jeans and a T-shirt, and he had locs. I remember reading an article about him years ago that talked about how he had so much power in his feet that he didn't have to lift them very high to make such a loud noise, and that he had a different sense of rhythm because he was coming through hip-hop. Those other guys, they came up through jazz. So their style was more of a jazz style. But Savion, all percussion. It just made sense to use Savion as the method for teaching it.

10. What was your intention behind Keith's name? Is there a reason why it was important to have this particular horn player in the band?

You know, the simple answer, which is the honest answer, is because a girl can be named Keith, and a girl can play the trumpet. There's not really much more to it. Oh, and the guys can still have a crush on her. Whether she cares or not is up to her, but she can be all of who she is and allow the world to deal with their feelings about it. By the way, this is exactly how I felt about Sheila E.

11. Besides the protagonist Stuy, is there a character that you relate to the most? Why?

Dunks. Not because of his upbringing—I didn't grow up rich or anything like that—but because of his imagination. The desire for strangeness and the passion for stretching and reaching for something that feels far away and yet feels so close, right? And he's kind of all over the place, and I'm kind of all over the place too. That's my guy. Shout out to Dunks.

12. *Soundtrack* was first published as an audiobook. What was your reaction when you first heard it?

It was beautiful and it was far beyond what I could have imagined.

ACKNOWLEDGMENTS

There are so many people I owe gratitude to as it pertains to the inspiration and execution of this project, most of whom I haven't spoken to in over a decade. These brilliant artists I shared couches, futons, bodega dinners, and train rides with, as we tried to figure out what our rhythms were. What our song was. What it meant to live an expressive life. Folks like Zamani, and Myisha, and Jahmed, and Chenits, and Radha. Like all the subway buskers whose names I never knew, but whose music I'll always remember. The old man with the scratchy voice on the A train, singing Bob Marley songs. Or the doo-wop group who usually camped out at a downtown F train stop, crooning my mother's music. Or the conga players who would crowd into the subway cars to add heartbeat to the metallic pulse of the journey. Thank you all.

To New York City, thank you. I'll never be able to repay you (but you always make me try!).

And lastly, I have to thank the folks who were hands-on, like my agent, Elena Giovinazzo, for keeping this book in the chamber. Everything finds its place. Thank you to Dan Zitt, Brian Ramcharan, Alexandra Hernandez, Kate Smith, and the entire Listening Library team for unearthing this story. I'm forever grateful. And to Phoebe Yeh and Crown Books, for having the vision to take this thing even further.

Thank you all!

And now, a drum solo!

DISCUSSION QUESTIONS

1. Read the epigraph by Michael Jackson: "Let the madness in the music get to you, life ain't so bad at all . . ." Why did Jason Reynolds use this quote at the beginning of the novel?

2. The narrator Stuy plays the drums. Why is he passionate about being a drummer? Who was his first teacher? How was he taught to drum?

3. Compare and contrast Stuy's relationships with his mom and his uncle. How would you describe each relationship? How do they both shape Stuy as he grows up?

4. Besides Stuy, who are the other musicians in *Soundtrack*? What instruments do they play? How did they learn their craft? How do their personalities inform their music?

5. Which character do you relate to the most? Why?

6. Stuy and Dunks form a band. So do Alexis and Keith. How are the bands alike? How are they different? How does music help them deal with the challenges in their lives?

7. Compare Stuy's, Dunks's, and Alexis's relationships with their respective families. What are other examples of family in *Soundtrack*? What is the author saying about found families?

8. How is *Soundtrack* a New York story? What makes the characters New York kids? What makes Soundtrack a New York band?

9. Stuy discovers that Dom, his mom's boyfriend, hits his mom. So Alexis decides to help Stuy teach Dom a lesson, but Alexis gets arrested for assault. Stuy hopes the band money will convince Dom to drop his charges. Did Stuy and Alexis make the right decisions? How do friends show their loyalty?

10. What does Famous Frankie do for the band? When Frankie says, "We make music. We make magic," what does he mean?

11. Listen to the *Soundtrack* audiobook. How is this experience different from reading the novel?

12. What is the author saying about listening to music and playing music? Is music or art a part of your life?

ABOUT THE AUTHOR

JASON REYNOLDS is the #1 *New York Times* bestselling author of more than twenty books for children and young adults. A 2024 MacArthur Fellow, Jason is best known for his novels, including the *New York Times* bestseller *Twenty-Four Seconds from Now . . .*, which received the Coretta Scott King Author Award and seven starred reviews; *Long Way Down*, which received Newbery, Printz, and Coretta Scott King honors; *All American Boys* (co-written with Brendan Kiely), which received a Coretta Scott King Author Honor and the Walter Dean Myers Award for Outstanding Children's Literature; and the Track series, of which the first book, *Ghost*, was a finalist for the National Book Award for Young People's Literature. For more on Jason, visit him on Instagram at @jasonreynolds83 and at JasonWritesBooks.com.

LISTEN TO THE AUDIOBOOK!

Featuring original music by Grammy-winning composer Justin Ellington, and special effects!

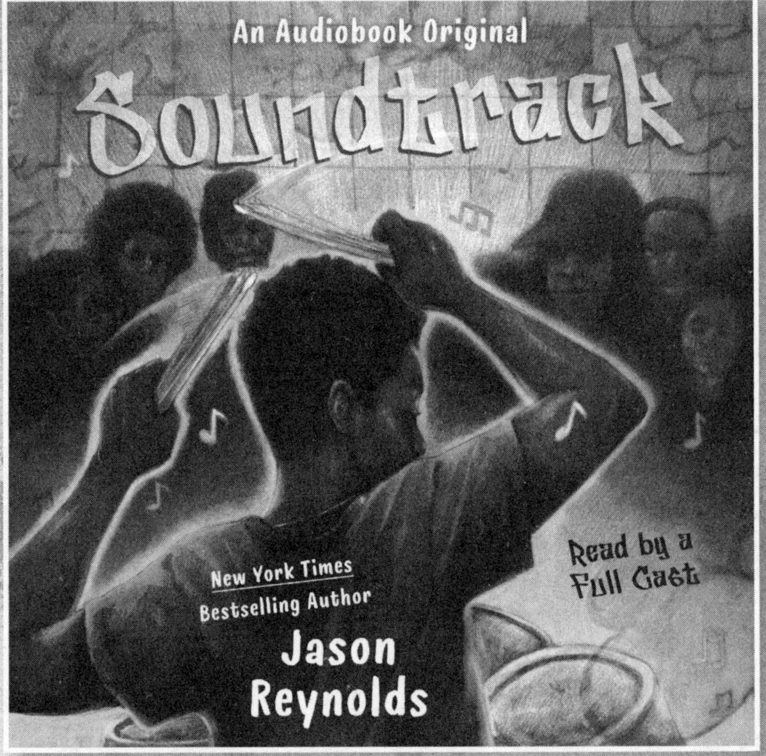

"Justin Ellington's extensive and essential musical score gives *Soundtrack* its soundtrack. The result is a production full of heart."

—*AudioFile Magazine*

Spotify Best Audiobook of the Year

Apple Books Must Listen

AudioFile Magazine Earphone Award Winner